Liam pulled the towel from her

Alix wanted to protest, but the words wouldn't come. She was watching him watching her, and she knew an unquenchable excitement.

His hands closed on her waist, traveling downward until they rested on the curve of her hips. His gaze touched hers, then dropped slowly to her lips and down to her breasts, barely concealed by the tiny jade-green bikini. Then his mouth brushed hers gently, and she swayed forward.

Liam must have been aware of her arousal, for he laid a trail of little kisses on her eyelids, her temples, the corners of her mouth. Alix was trembling as she fought to retain her sanity. She had been kissed before but never with this slow insidious beguilement that was transforming her shaking body into one long ache of yearning.

SARA CRAVEN
is also the author of these

Harlequin Presents

and this

Harlequin Romance

Many of these books are available at your local bookseller.

For a free catalog listing all titles currently available,
send your name and address to:

HARLEQUIN READER SERVICE
1440 South Priest Drive, Tempe, AZ 85281
Canadian address: Stratford, Ontario N5A 6W2

SARA CRAVEN

unguarded moment

Harlequin Books

TORONTO • NEW YORK • LOS ANGELES • LONDON
AMSTERDAM • PARIS • SYDNEY • HAMBURG
STOCKHOLM • ATHENS • TOKYO • MILAN

Harlequin Presents first edition December 1982
ISBN 0-373-10551-7

Original hardcover edition published in 1982
by Mills & Boon Limited

CHAPTER ONE

As the taxi stopped, so did the rain, and Alix Coulter flung the sky an appreciative glance as she paid off the driver. Her three weeks in the sun had been a leisurely delight, but at the same time had spoilt her for the vagaries of the English climate in August. It had been a distinct let-down to descend on London through thick cloud and find a sullen, humid day waiting for her.

Driving through the glistening streets, she'd wondered half humorously, half apprehensively, whether the threatening weather was an indication of what was waiting for her. Bianca had been all smiles when she'd said *'Au revoir'*, but that was no guarantee that Alix would be equally warmly welcomed. Bianca's moods were—mercurial, to find the kindest way of putting it, Alix supposed. Even the slightest obstacle in her primrose path could bring on a tantrum which might last for days. 'Artistic temperament', the directors and producers who worked with her on her films tactfully called it. 'Sheer bloodymindedness' was the more down-to-earth description from Lester Marchant, Bianca's most recent husband, now licking his wounds and ruefully contemplating the divorce settlement in the United States.

Alix sighed a little. She had liked Lester, and was sorry when he finally declared enough was enough and moved out. But as she was the first to admit, it wasn't easy being a member of Bianca's entourage. She had worked for Bianca for three years now, and while it was undoubtedly exciting, it wasn't always enjoyable.

Alix had often wondered, especially when Bianca was being more than usually imperious, why she stood it. She was a good secretary. She was calm, efficient and well organised. She wouldn't have the slightest difficulty in finding another job—and an employer not nearly as trying and demanding as Bianca apparently took a delight in being. And yet she still stayed, restoring order to Bianca's hectic social life, smoothing out her travel arrangements, taking her frequent changes of mind in her stride as equably as she did Bianca's constant changes of clothes.

It must be family feeling, she told herself wryly.

She had been quite shattered to learn that Bianca Layton was her aunt, her own mother's sister. She could never remember hearing it referred to even once during her childhood, although Bianca was already a name in films on both sides of the Atlantic, celebrated for her outrageous beauty and her love affairs which sometimes, but not always, ended in marriage.

It was incredible even to think of Bianca coming from the same staid background as her mother. All her life Margaret Coulter had stood up for all the virtues that Bianca seemed deliberately to flout. Alix often wondered whether her mother had been ashamed or envious of her amazingly glamorous sibling.

When Alix had at last discovered the truth, learned that Bianca Layton was her aunt and was coming to visit them, she had appealed to her mother, 'But why did you never tell me? Why have you never said anything all these years?'

Margaret Coulter was a quiet woman, but now she was so silent that Alix was afraid she had offended her in some way.

At last she said, 'There seemed no reason for you to know. Her world isn't ours, and I never thought we would ever see her again.'

There was a note in her voice which told Alix quite unequivocally that it was Margaret herself who had desired the separation. She looked at her mother uncertainly, at the greying dark hair cut and waved neatly into the same style for the past ten years, at the figure, no longer youthfully slender but blurring into comfortable lines, and realised that Margaret was probably dreading the inevitable comparisons which would be made.

Margaret met her gaze and her smile was wintry. 'No, we're not alike,' she said. 'We never were. No one took us for sisters, even when we were at school. Sometimes I could hardly believe it myself.'

It had seemed even more unbelievable when Bianca finally arrived. She seemed to fill the house with her presence. Her perfume hung exotically in the air. She was charm, she glittered, and she never once by either word or deed gave any indication that she found her sister's home and her sister's family drearily suburban and middle class.

She was gracious in a remote way to Alix and to Debbie, her younger sister. She obviously wasn't used to very young girls; all three of her marriages had been childless.

And when Bianca had departed as dramatically as she had come, and they were left with that inevitable feeling of anticlimax, Debbie had said, 'But why did she come? What did she want?'

But no one had an answer to that—at least not then. Sometimes Alix found herself staring at the place at the neatly set table with its embroidered cloth and matching china where Bianca had sat and wondering dazedly whether it had all really happened, or whether they hadn't been victims of some sort of mass hallucination, or one of those dreams where the Queen comes to tea as if she was an old friend.

It had been a fleeting visit, and yet it seemed to have had a profound effect. Margaret Coulter had never been the ebullient, extrovert type, but now she seemed to become more withdrawn than ever, and her family watched her with concern.

One night Alix, who couldn't sleep, came downstairs for a drink of water and heard her father's voice, almost coaxing.

'Don't worry, Meg. It's over. It's past.'

And her mother's response, her tone throbbing with something like hatred, 'Or it could be just beginning.'

Alix, unseen and unheard, went back to bed without her drink, instinct telling her that any sort of intrusion would be unwelcome.

What had her mother meant? she wondered as she tossed and turned restlessly. Aunt Bianca had said nothing about another visit. Was this what her mother was afraid of? Constant descents on them, like some goddess coming down from Olympus, with all the fuss and attendant publicity which would probably be inevitable? She could understand why quiet, conventional Margaret should find such an idea abhorrent. It was that unmistakable note of venom which disturbed her. Her mother was a good woman—everyone said so. She belonged to the Mothers' Union and raised money for Oxfam and a string of other charities. She didn't have an enemy in the world—or at least that was what Alix had always believed.

She could only surmise that at some time in the dim and distant past something had happened between the sisters which had driven them irrevocably apart. There had been a breach which Bianca's unexpected visit had done nothing to heal. On the contrary, old wounds seemed to be open and bleeding.

Gradually, as the weeks lengthened into months, and nothing was heard from Bianca, although plenty was heard about her—more films, another marriage—things began to return to normal.

And two years had passed before Bianca came back into their lives again.

'Cheer up, ducks. It may never happen.' The taxi-driver's cheerful voice cut across her reverie, and Alix started. He had unloaded her luggage, two cases in cream hide, on to the pavement beside her. 'Very nice too.' His gaze slid from the cases over Alix, and on to the house they were standing outside, so she wasn't altogether sure what he was referring to, and certainly not inclined to ask.

The tan she had acquired over the past few weeks suited her, she knew, and she was wearing her thick dark hair loose on her shoulders instead of in a neat chignon as she usually did. Although that, of course, was not entirely her own choice. It was just that Bianca preferred her to look neat and businesslike when she was working.

Well, perhaps not just that, Alix admitted to herself wryly. She remembered the first day she had come here, summoned by a telephone call not from Bianca herself but from Lester Marchant.

Would she come and see them, he had said, because he had a proposition to put to her. Alix had hesitated at first, her instinct telling her that her mother wouldn't want her to go. But her curiosity proved too strong in the end.

She could remember the uncertainty she had felt, standing at the foot of the steps for the first time, looking up at the tall Georgian house and wondering if she had the courage to ring the doorbell.

At least she didn't have to do that any more, she thought, as she fitted her key into the lock, and she was certainly a more confident and self-reliant person than she would have been if she'd gone on with her humdrum little job in a solicitor's office.

The driver carried her cases in and she thanked him with a tip and a smile he would remember far longer. Then she closed the door and stood looking around her with the usual pang of delight which assailed her every time she entered the house. It was a beautiful hall, broad and spacious, with a broad imposing staircase, and the walls panelled in honey-coloured wood. Bianca had other houses, but this was where she spent most of her time.

'In spite of everything, England is still the most civilised place to be,' she was fond of saying in interviews. The only thing she didn't find civilised was the weather, and as autumn dwindled into winter with rain and fog and frost, she was generally ready to be off to her home in California, or to accept any of the numerous invitations to friends' villas in Marbella or the South of France.

Alix had seen a lot of the world in the past few years. She had expected to be taken on location when Bianca was filming, but she hadn't been sure about the trips which were really frivolity. But Bianca had dismissed her misgivings with an impatient wave of her hand. When she travelled, she liked her entourage with her, and that included Alix as well as Edith Montgomery who had been with her all her life, it seemed, fulfilling a variety of roles—a kind of companion-maid-masseuse-dresser-housekeeper rolled into one.

Monty was coming downstairs now, neat in the dark skirt and white tailored shirt she usually wore, and she looked at Alix with her brows raised.

'So you're back,' she observed grudgingly and unnecessarily.

Alix kept her face straight. When she had first come to work here, she had been unnerved by Monty's inexplicable but thinly veiled hostility. Later, when she became more settled, she had been able to reason it out. Monty wasn't a young woman. Her face was thin and lined, and she made no attempt to disguise the liberal streaks of grey in her hair. But she had a close relationship with Bianca, and perhaps she thought having her niece working as a secretary and actually living in the house might be a threat to that relationship. Alix had had to walk on eggshells for several months in an attempt to convince Monty that she had nothing to worry about, that although she had accepted the job she wasn't trying to muscle in on anything else. She supposed she had succeeded up to a point. They had achieved a kind of armed truce, but she had stopped hoping that Monty would regard her with any real warmth or approval.

Now she smiled more widely than she felt inclined to do, and said, 'Yes, I am. How are things? Any crises during my absence?'

'We've had our ups and downs,' Monty said drily. 'But you're just in time for the row of the year.'

'Oh, hell!' Alix was apprehensive. 'It isn't the film, surely? It hasn't fallen through?'

'No, that's still very much on the cards. Veronese is coming over here shortly to talk to her about it.' Monty paused heavily. 'No, it's this biography.'

'Oh?' Alix's voice sharpened. This was something she hadn't foreseen. Before she'd gone away, Bianca had been all for the suggestion that her life story should be written. She had even had boxes of ancient photographs brought down from the attic to look for suitable prints of herself as baby and small child for the inevitable illustrations. 'What's gone wrong?'

'They don't want her to write it.' Monty gave a resigned shrug. 'She thought it would simply be a matter of hiring someone to listen to her talk through her reminiscences, and then ghost them, but now it seems the publishers have commissioned someone—a Liam Brant. Have you heard of him?'

Alix thought she had, but couldn't remember in what connection.

She said, 'What has she got against him?'

'He isn't her idea. She wanted that girl—the one who did the article about her in *Woman of Today*. She thought she was *simpatico*.'

'It was certainly a very flattering article,' Alix said drily. 'I doubt if the same note of unquestioning admiration could be sustained for a whole book. Has she met this Mr Brant? Perhaps he's *simpatico* too.'

'He's coming here this morning.' Monty sounded dour. 'And she says she won't see him. A nice start that is!'

A nice start indeed, Alix thought resignedly, bidding her holiday goodbye for ever. She was back in the thick of it, and no mistake.

She lifted the dark fall of hair wearily from her neck. 'If he's the publishers' choice, then we may be stuck with him, unless she can come up with a better reason for turning him down than she'd rather it was someone else. And it won't do to antagonise him. I'll talk to her.'

'I wish you would,' said Monty, and that was an admission coming from her. She sounded tired, Alix thought. Perhaps the last three weeks had been more trying than usual, although after all these years Monty should be used to Bianca's vagaries. 'Leave your cases. I'll get Harris to see to them.'

Harris and his wife occupied a small flat in the basement. They took care of the house when Bianca was away, and when she was in residence, Harris was a total manservant, doing most of the fetching and carrying around the household, but acting as butler when the occasion demanded, while Mrs Harris was a divine cook.

They had worked for Bianca for a long time too, and they seemed impervious to the storms which periodically rocked the household, or perhaps they stayed because the wages were good, and the perfect employer didn't exist anyway, Alix sometimes thought, amused.

She ran upstairs and paused outside the door of Bianca's first floor suite, wondering whether to knock. Bianca usually catnapped during the morning, and she hated being caught doing it. But even as Alix hesitated, she heard the unmistakable crash of shattering glass coming from behind the door. She smiled grimly, turned the handle and went into the room.

'I do hope that wasn't a mirror,' she said lightly. 'I don't think we can do with seven years' bad luck.'

It was a vase of flowers. Broken glass, water and sad-looking blooms were strewn across the carpet at Bianca's feet. Alix thought detachedly that she looked magnificent, even if the flush in her cheeks was caused by temper rather than excitement or good health.

The huge emerald eyes, which had been staring straight ahead, focussed on Alix and sharpened.

Bianca said, 'So it's you. Where the hell have you been?'

Alix suppressed a sigh. 'So nice to be needed,' she said drily. 'I've been on holiday, in case you've forgotten—to Rhodes. Didn't you get my card?'

'I may have done,' Bianca gave an irritable shrug. 'The girl they sent from the agency has been dealing with the mail. My God, what a mistake that was!'

'Wasn't she any good?' Alix fetched a discarded newspaper from the table beside the chaise-longue and began to gather the broken glass and wilted flowers on to it.

'Useless. It's all her fault that this frightful man is coming here this morning. She made the appointment without consulting me. Well, you'll just have to get rid of him, Alix. Telephone him. Tell him I'm ill—tell him anything. I won't see him. I won't!' There was an hysterical note in Bianca's voice and Alix glanced up at her, her brows drawing together in a faint frown.

She said equably, 'Very well. But what shall I say when he asks for another appointment? And he surely will. This is a commission, and he won't want to lose out.'

Bianca's perfectly painted mouth twisted sullenly. 'Oh God, you sound just like Seb! He won't help at all. He says I've agreed that my life story should be written, and the best thing I can do is co-operate.' She swore viciously. 'Some public relations man he turned out to be!'

'He's one of the best,' Alix said, faintly amused. 'And his advice is probably good.'

Bianca gestured wildly. 'But I don't want his advice. I

just want him to get rid of this terrible man—this Brant.'

Alix retrieved a sliver of glass from the carpet with a certain amount of care.

'How do you know he's so terrible? He might be charming. If you met him you might like him.'

'I would not.' Bianca made it sound like a solemn vow. 'He writes the most awful things. He did the Kristen Wallace book last year, and he made her sound like a neurotic bitch.'

'Well, isn't she?' In spite of her care, Alix had cut her finger on a splinter, and she sucked the blood reflectively.

'Of course,' Bianca said impatiently. 'But he had no right to say so.'

Alix hadn't read the book, but she could remember Bianca doing so with gurgles of enjoyment, and she knew now why the name seemed familiar. The Wallace biography had caused a sensation because it had exploded a myth once and for all. Kristen Wallace had acquired a reputation for playing serious roles in films which relied heavily on prolonged silences and heavy symbolism for their impact. In the book, Kristen had been encouraged to talk about her work, which she had done at length, revealing in the process that she hadn't, in all probability, understood one word of the deeply significant lines she was called on to say. The real genius, it had been suggested, was Miss Wallace's dialogue coach. Alix remembered one critic had called the book, 'A devastating insight into a deeply trivial mind.' One thing was certain: Kristen Wallace had been a laughing stock afterwards, and she hadn't made a film since.

'He's a hatchet man—a real swine,' Bianca railed. 'I don't want that kind of thing written about me.'

Alix began to smile. She said, 'That's hardly likely. You're not a pretentious idiot like La Wallace.'

'I don't want anyone like that poking about in my private life,' Bianca said with finality.

One answer to that was that there was no aspect of Bianca's life which could be considered private, but Alix wasn't brave enough to suggest it. Her affairs, her marriages, and her divorces had all been conducted in the full glare of the publicity spotlight. There could be few details about them that the great reading public didn't already know, *ad nauseam*.

'So you'll telephone him now,' Bianca persisted. 'And when you've done that, you can phone Seb and tell him he's fired.'

'Just as you say,' Alix agreed cheerfully. There was no problem about the last instruction. Seb had a fireproof contract, and he was used to Bianca's tempers. He said they added further colour to life's rich tapestry.

She disposed of the broken glass and flowers, and told Monty regretfully about the soaked carpet, then went off to the room she used as an office.

The agency girl might have roused Bianca's ire, but she seemed to be a neat worker. The desk was immaculate, and the carbons of the correspondence she had dealt with were all clipped together by the typewriter so Alix could familiarise herself with everything that had happened while she was away.

The filing had all been done too, and she found Liam Brant's letter without difficulty. It was a polite enough request for an interview, she thought, as she dialled his number, but the signature was a give-away—a slash of black ink, harsh and arrogant, across the creamy paper.

His line was engaged, so she re-dialled and spoke to Seb.

'You're fired.'

'That's the fourth time this year,' Seb said mournfully. 'One day I'll take her at her word, and then where will she be? And how are you, my honey flower? Did you enjoy your happy hols?'

'I wish I could remember,' Alix sighed. 'I've now got to gently but firmly get rid of Mr Brant.'

There was a startled sound, then Seb said, 'I can tell

you now that you won't. I tried to indicate that to
Bianca, but there was no reasoning with her. She put
the phone down on me in a hell of a rage.'

'And broke a vase,' Alix said ruefully. 'I've just been
picking the pieces up.'

'Well, my advice is still to co-operate with Mr Brant,
or you may have more than the pieces of a vase to pick
up,' Seb assured her. 'Have you come across any of his
books?'

'Only by hearsay. I gather Bianca's been reading some
of them—the Kristen Wallace biography in particular.'

'Well, I suggest you read them too, so that you know
what you're up against.'

When she had replaced the receiver, Alix sat for a
moment or two staring at the phone as if it might bite
her. Then slowly and carefully she re-dialled Liam
Brant's number. She did not know whether to be sorry
or relieved when it was still engaged.

She looked at the internal telephone on her desk,
wondering if she should ring Bianca's suite to warn her
she had been unable to get through to Liam Brant as
yet, or whether she should go up and tell her in person,
passing on at the same time Seb's rather terse advice.

She needed to go upstairs anyway. She had her unpacking to do, and she needed to change. Bianca had
been too overwrought to notice her brief cream denim
skirt and sleeveless black top, and her bare tanned legs
culminating in flimsy leather sandals bought from a
street market, but she would notice eventually, and not
be pleased.

When Alix had first come to work there, she had been
so dazzled to find herself the possessor of a salary which
exceeded anything she could reasonably have hoped for
that she had plunged into an orgy of buying. She didn't
want the way-out things displayed in so many of the
boutiques, but it was fun to choose things which
enhanced her young slenderness, clothes which whispered to her entranced image in fitting room mirrors

that she could be more than merely attractive—that she might even have the promise of beauty.

She had entirely forgotten what had happened after her first visit to the house, when she had been brought into this very room to meet her predecessor, whose abrupt departure had provided the reason for her being offered the job.

The girl had been tight-lipped and hostile, and Alix had been unsure how to defuse the situation, wishing very much that Lester Marchant who had brought her here and introduced them had remained to ease the way for her. But of course he hadn't, she thought, her mouth lifting in a smile of wry reminiscence. Lester had problems of his own, even then.

'So you're the new secretary.' The other girl had surveyed her from head to toe. 'I don't think you'll last long. You're not bad looking and Bianca doesn't brook any possible rivals, you know. That's why I'm going. I could handle the job, but someone bothered to give me a word and a smile at one of her cocktail parties when he should have been devoting all his attention to her, and that's fatal.'

Hot with embarrassment, Alix said, 'Perhaps you ought to know that Miss Layton is my aunt.'

'She is?' The other girl sounded astonished, rather than abashed. 'Well, that's probably the last time you'll ever be allowed to tell anyone that. And it won't save you from the limitations Bianca likes to put on her staff. Niece or not, you'll submit to the image she wants, or you'll be out. Now, I suppose I'd better show you how the filing system works.'

Alix had been too dazed by the harshness of the words to pay much attention to the demonstration that followed. She was torn with doubts anyway, knowing how her mother would react to the news that she had accepted a post as Bianca's secretary, however high-powered and well paid, and beyond the wildest dreams of anyone as relatively young and inexperienced as she was. Whatever the trouble was between Bianca and her mother, she had an uneasy feeling that her decision to work for Bianca, to live in her house, to devote her waking hours to her interests, would improve nothing between the sisters.

Now, it seemed, she would have problems at work as well as at home. She had known a momentary impulse to cut and run, but now an older, wiser Alix knew that she would have regretted it bitterly if she had done so.

Even a few weeks afterwards when Bianca, her smiling lips belying her narrowed eyes, had suggested charmingly that perhaps some of her new clothes were more suitable to her leisure hours rather than an office environment, she had learned to swallow her humiliation. Because by that time she knew that nothing—not Bianca's moods, or Monty's hostility, or the silences at home which disturbed her most of all—could persuade her to abandon the sheer stimulation of her new job. And if Bianca wanted her hair tied demurely back instead of flowing freely over her shoulders, and preferred her to dress in quiet drab styles, which were both businesslike and unobtrusive, then she would not argue. It might be weak-willed, but Bianca was paying the piper, and handsomely too, and Alix had no real objection to her calling the tune.

So she dressed and behaved with the utmost discretion, and she made no men friends where she might conceivably be accused of poaching on Bianca's preserves.

She told herself that she didn't really mind either that Bianca had fulfilled her predecessor's prophecy by describing Alix airily as a young cousin, explaining later, 'A niece sounds incredibly ageing, darling. Don't you agree?'

Alix was realistic enough to know that even if she had objected violently, it would really have made no difference. Bianca spent a lot of her time pampering her face and body, keeping the march of time at bay. It would have been hard at any time to guess her age, and Bianca clearly intended to keep people guessing for many years yet.

She tried Liam Brant's number once more for luck, and grimaced as the engaged signal came steadily to her ears.

'Talkative devil, aren't you?' she addressed him as she put the phone down.

As she crossed the hall, the doorbell rang, and she hesitated, wondering if she should answer it, but she could already hear Harris's footsteps as he came up the basement stairs, and besides, Bianca wouldn't thank her for receiving guests in her holiday gear. So she went on towards the stairs, returning a smiling greeting to Harris' hearty, 'Good morning, miss. A pleasure to see you, if I may say so.'

Of course he could say so, she thought, as she put her hand on the curve of the banister rail. He was the only one who had said anything of the sort, and it was nice to be welcomed.

She was still smiling when she turned slightly to see who was at the door. He was tall, and his shadow fell across the watery sunlight which was making a brave attempt to straggle across the hall floor.

His voice was low-pitched, resonant and cool. 'My name's Brant. Miss Layton is expecting me.'

As he spoke, he glanced across the hall and his eyes fell on Alix, standing transfixed on the stairs.

She looked back at him blankly, registering his lean height, the darkness of his hair, the arrogant strength of nose, mouth and chin, and the cynically amused appreciation in his eyes as he surveyed her.

Her first thought was, 'My God, it can't be him! He's on the phone. He can't be here.' Her second was, 'Bianca will kill me!'

And she went on up the stairs, not looking back, but aware just the same that he was still watching her, and having hell's own job not to break into a run and take

Bianca's elegant stairs two at a time.

She flew into her bedroom, nearly falling over her holiday cases which Harris had put there. Holiday gear was the last thing she wanted now, she thought, kicking off her sandals and shrugging the too-revealing black top over her head. She grabbed the nearest dress, a neat shirtwaister in beige cotton, and pulled it on, forcing the buttons through the holes, and knotting the tie belt hastily, before sliding her feet into matching low-heeled pumps. There was not time to fix her hair properly, she decided, gathering it firmly into a swirl at the back of her head, and anchoring it with a few well-placed hairpins.

And it was no use bothering Bianca at this stage. She would go downstairs and face the wretched man and see if she could persuade him to go away until she and Seb and Leon, Bianca's agent, had had a chance to talk to her, to reason with her.

Harris was waiting at the foot of the stairs. 'I've shown the gentleman into the drawing room, Miss Alix. Shall I bring coffee? And shall I tell Miss Layton he's here.'

'Not for the time being.' Alix's heart was thumping in a most uncharacteristic way, and the headlong rush to change into an approximation of what Bianca expected of her had made her breathless. 'I—I'll ring if I want anything.'

She paused at the drawing room door, took a deep steadying breath, then turned the handle and went in, pinning a small cool smile to her lips.

He was standing by the fireplace, glancing through one of the magazines, usually arranged neatly on the sofa table.

He looked at Alix, and his dark brows lifted. 'So,' he said. 'The little niece.'

It was desperately important not to appear thrown, but she was. There had never been the slightest hint of her real relationship to Bianca in any of the hundreds of thousands of words which had been written about her aunt, so how in the world did he know?

'Don't bother to deny it,' he added, his voice drawling as it invaded her appalled silence. 'You're rather like her—as she was when she was younger, anyway.'

Oh no, Alix thought. He mustn't. He really must not meet Bianca ever, if this is a fair sample of the kind of thing he says.

She lifted her chin and gave him back stare for stare. 'How kind of you to say so, Mr Brant.' She allowed her own voice to drawl slightly. 'And you've done your homework well.'

'I'm paid to do so, Miss Coulter—or may I call you Alix, as we seem destined to spend a considerable amount of time in each other's company over the next few months.'

'Over my dead body,' Alix said silently. She said coolly, 'Miss Layton prefers a certain measure of formality in her business dealings, Mr Brant. As a matter of fact, I've been trying to telephone you for the past hour.'

'My phone's out of order.' He gave her a level look. 'I hope you weren't trying to tell me that Miss Layton would be unable to keep our appointment because she's been laid low by some virus.'

As this was exactly the excuse Alix had been desperately formulating, she had to grind her teeth.

'Miss Layton is perfectly well,' she said stiffly. 'Nevertheless, it won't be convenient for her to see you today. That was what I was trying to tell you. I'm very sorry.'

'Now that I doubt.' He tossed the magazine impatiently down on to the table again, and gave her a frowning look. 'I never saw less evidence of regret in anybody. Let's have the truth, Miss Coulter. Your aunt has developed cold feet over the whole project, hasn't she, and she's delegated you to break the bad news to me.'

Anger sparked in Alix. 'You're very astute, Mr Brant. Under the circumstances I don't think there's any need to extend this interview further.' She turned away, but incredibly he was beside her, his hand on her arm, detaining her.

'Then think again, secretary bird. I am a professional man, and I don't like having my time deliberately wasted.'

'Then you'd better send us a bill,' Alix flared. 'Is your profession paid by the hour, or the minute?' She gave her watch a studied look. 'Of which I calculate you've wasted approximately fifteen. Unless you walked here, of course.'

His smile held no amusement whatever. 'Your sharp tongue doesn't match your demure exterior, secretary bird. I've been commissioned to write this book about Bianca Layton, and I intend to do so, with her co-operation, or without it if I have to.'

'Did Kristen Wallace co-operate?' Alix asked. 'It didn't make a great deal of difference in the end. You still did a hatchet job on her.'

'I didn't have to, Miss Coulter. The lady was only too ready to rush headlong on her doom. All I had to do was make a truthful record of her idiocies.'

'Oh, I'm sure you have a great concern with the truth,' she said scornfully.

He lifted a shoulder almost wearily. 'I've never found lying to be of any great benefit. Your aunt's attitude puzzles me, I confess. Less than a week ago she was apparently full of enthusiasm about the book. Now she's changed her mind, and it makes me wonder why.'

'The waning of her enthusiasm dates from her discovery that you were involved.' Alix was suddenly aware he was still holding her arm, and angrily shook herself free. 'She's entitled to deny you the right to invade her privacy.'

'Privacy?' He looked faintly amused. 'Since when has Bianca Layton valued that commodity? She's lived her life well and truly in the public eye. She knows what her public expects, and she doesn't short-change them. I'd have said her life was—an open book already, wouldn't you. And yet suddenly she's wary. It makes me wonder. It really makes me wonder.'

'Makes you wonder about what?' Alix demanded sharply.

He smiled down into her flushed indignant face. 'Just what she has to hide? What else? Now, as it's clear you have no intention of letting me see her today, I'll go, but I shall be back, and it would be better if next time she was prepared to see me.'

'Threats, Mr Brant?' Alix felt her voice quiver slightly.

'Call it a friendly warning,' he said pleasantly. '*Au revoir*, Miss Coulter. Oh, by the way——' his hand reached out, incredibly, and unfastened the top button on her dress, then moved down to the next, 'in the interests of keeping our business relationship formal, perhaps you ought to take a little more care in the way you dress.'

'How dare you!' Her face burning, Alix stepped back. 'There's nothing the matter with my clothes.'

'That's open to debate. What I was actually trying to indicate was that somewhere along the way you've put a button through the wrong hole.'

Glancing down at the front of her dress, she was chagrined to see that he was correct.

'Thank you,' she said icily. 'I can put it right for myself.'

'As you please,' he shrugged. 'Don't overreact, Miss Coulter. There's no need to make like a frightened virgin. Buttoned or unbuttoned, you're simply not my type, so you're in no danger of imminent rape. I hope that reassures you.'

Reassures me? Alix wanted to scream. Nothing about you reassures me. I want you out of this house, and out of our lives.

Aloud, she said with emphasis, 'Goodbye, Mr Brant.'

He shook his head. 'No, Miss Coulter. Didn't you hear me say I'd be back?'

He inclined his head to her with mocking courtesy, then reached past her to open the drawing-room door.

Alix watched him cross the hall to the front door. It wasn't until it closed behind him that she realised she had been holding her breath.

Whatever happened, she told herself fiercely, no matter what Seb or anyone else said, she was going to keep that—character assassin with his insinuations and innuendoes away from Bianca. Whatever her faults, she didn't deserve anyone like Liam Brant casting a spotlight on them. Bianca needed to be protected from him, and she, Alix, would see that it was done.

She swallowed, and her hand moved slowly and reluctantly to adjust the buttons on her dress. *'You're not my type,'* he'd told her cynically, and he certainly wasn't hers, so why could she not dismiss the memory of that brief brush of his fingers against her breasts?

Alix bit her lip. She was going to protect Bianca—but the unanswerable question was—who was going to protect her?

CHAPTER TWO

BIANCA was dressing to go out to lunch, and she was less than pleased to hear what Alix had to tell her.

'You seem to have handled it very badly,' she remarked tartly. 'I told you to get rid of him, not antagonise him.'

Alix groaned inwardly. 'I've been trying to explain,' she said. 'I don't think it's possible to do one without the other. He's absolutely determined to do the book, whether you agree or not.'

'We'll see about that.' Bianca's lips were tightly compressed.

Alix sighed. 'Is it really so impossible? After all, forewarned is forearmed, and according to Seb it's better to have him on your side.'

'Oh, Seb,' Bianca said with scorn. 'A lot of good he's been in all this. Why should I agree to this book? God knows I don't need the publicity. I already have more scripts lined up than I'll ever have time to do.'

She added some gloss to her lips.

'There is nothing to stop anyone, any time, writing a book about you,' Alix pointed out patiently. 'It's surprising really that no one's thought of doing it before. As I see it, if you refuse to have anything to do with it, you're deliberately forfeiting any control you might have over the content.'

Bianca swivelled round on her dressing stool. 'You sound as if you're on this man's side!'

'That's the last thing I am,' Alix muttered vehemently. 'But he worries me.'

'I can't imagine why he should.' Bianca was still watching her, her brows raised curiously. 'I should be worried, if anyone is. Why should you be so concerned?'

Alix met her gaze steadily. 'I hardly know. Perhaps it could have something to do with the fact that you're a blood relation as well as my employer.'

'How very touching!' Bianca's lip curled. 'Well, don't fret on my behalf, darling child. I can take care of myself.'

Alix felt a full flush creep into her face. There was a bite in Bianca's tone which was bound to hurt. It was one of the things she had never been able to understand. She supposed Bianca had offered the job in the first place because she was her niece, and therefore she could expect more than usual loyalty from her, and yet her aunt had never treated her as if she was a relation. Alix could never say that she had received any kind of indulgence from Bianca, and not much affection either. Any tentative attempts by Alix to infuse some warmth into their relationship had always been resisted.

Alix had learned to come to terms with it, of course, mainly by telling herself that this should be regarded as just another job, and that Bianca should be regarded as just another employer. In other circumstances she would expect only to do what she was paid for and accept her salary. Yet at the same time she was realistic enough to know that Bianca made demands on her which no stranger would ever accede to.

She had tried once to explain this to her mother, but Margaret Coulter's face had hardened.

'Did you really expect anything different?' she asked roughly. 'Bianca always did want to eat her cake and have it at the same time. She was selfish and unfeeling from the day she was born. She expected everything and everyone to revolve round her like—like satellites around a moon. And now you're caught too.'

Alix had been too shaken by the depth of feeling in her mother's voice to do more than offer a token protest, but afterwards she had wondered whether what

Margaret had said was true. Was she beguiled into acquiescence by the undoubted glamour of Bianca's personality? She was guiltily aware that she had been tactless in the way she had talked about her job at home. She tried unobtrusively from then on to demonstrate to Margaret that she still came first in her affections, but she wasn't altogether sure that she succeeded. In fact, the more she became absorbed in her job and its hectic demands, the farther she seemed to grow away from her family as a whole. Presumably they felt that someone who travelled the world in Bianca's wake might find the ups and downs of their everyday life less than fascinating, she thought wryly.

The most hurtful thing of all had been a few months ago when she had returned from California to find that nineteen-year-old Debbie was engaged, and that the party to celebrate it had been held in her absence.

She'd tried to pretend it didn't matter, to argue with herself that they couldn't have waited for her erratic timetable to bring her back to London again, but the pain lingered.

She often felt as if she occupied a kind of limbo. Her family had learned to live without her, had apparently closed the circle against her, and her only value to Bianca lay in her general efficiency and usefulness.

'I'll talk to Leon over lunch,' Bianca announced, scrutinising her flawless complexion through narrowed eyes. 'He should be able to think of something to get me off the hook.'

'I hope so,' Alix said with a sigh. 'Perhaps he'll be able to convince Mr Brant that you haven't anything to hide.'

'What on earth do you mean?' Bianca demanded sharply.

Alix met her eyes in the mirror. 'Oh, it was just something that he implied—that you didn't want him to write the book because there could be something you didn't want him to find out about.' She tried to smile rather uncertainly. 'I tried to tell him he was wrong, but

I'm not sure I was successful.' She broke off, uneasily, staring at Bianca's reflection, aware of a certain rigidity in her expression, and that the colour had faded in her face, emphasising the carefully applied blusher on her cheekbones.

Alix said sharply, 'Is something wrong? Surely there's nothing that he could find out . . .'

'Of course there's nothing,' Bianca snapped. 'I can't understand what's got into you, Alix. You're usually so level-headed and sensible, but this man seems to have sent your wits begging. Either that or going on holiday makes you lose all sense of proportion. You'd better take the rest of the day off and get a grip on yourself. I'll see you tomorrow.'

'Thanks,' Alix returned with a touch of irony. A small voice inside her head was saying that if Bianca retained her own sense of proportion about Liam Brant and the biography project, this whole situation would never have arisen, but of course she would never say so. 'I think I'll go home.'

'That will be nice.' Bianca turned away from the mirror, with a final look at her appearance. 'Give them all my best, won't you,' she added indifferently.

From the window, Alix watched Bianca climb into the waiting taxi and speed off to her lunch engagement with her agent. She could imagine the scene as Bianca entered the restaurant, see the admiring glances, hear the murmurs of recognition as she made her way to her table. Even a simple action like that became a performance, executed with the utmost confidence and panache.

And yet, a few minutes earlier, she had seen the mask slip. For a moment Bianca had been caught off balance, and Alix found herself wondering why, that indefinable sense of unease deepening. It was impossible, of course, that anyone who had lived her life as fully, and often as scandalously, revelling in the publicity, as Bianca could really have any kind of secret to conceal. She could have sworn that all Bianca's cupboards were open for inspection and lacking in skeletons of any kind.

At least I hope so, she thought as she turned away from the window.

Her first thought when she pushed open the back door and entered the kitchen was that her mother looked tired. But that could just be because she had been baking all morning for the local church's charity cake stall, she told herself.

'You've lost weight,' she teased as she hugged her mother.

'And not before time either,' Margaret said with a grimace. 'Just let me get this last batch out of the oven and I'll make us some tea.'

'That will be lovely.' Alix settled herself beside the kitchen table and stole a jam tart from the baking tray. 'No need to hurry. I have all day.'

'Oh dear!' Margaret looked at her quickly. 'I wish you'd telephoned, dear. You see, we're going out this evening to have a meal with Paul's parents—to talk over wedding details. Mrs Frensham's only expecting the three of us. I don't really see . . .'

'It doesn't matter,' Alix said quickly. 'I wouldn't dream of pushing in. I have loads of things to do, as it is—unpacking properly, for starters. And I wouldn't mind an early night. When is the wedding, or haven't they decided yet?'

'I think that's one of the things we're going to thrash out tonight. Both sides feel that they're rather young, but,' Margaret smiled fondly, 'I don't suppose they'll allow our opinions to carry too much weight. They're very much in love.'

'I'm glad for Debbie.' Alix meant it. Debbie had always been her cherished younger sister. 'I remember when we were children, she was always playing house. I was the one who was falling out of trees.'

'No, she never had your love of adventure. I suppose I always hoped that she would find a nice boy and settle down, so I can't really complain that she has done, even if it's rather sooner than I expected.'

'And what about me?' Alix suddenly wanted to cry. 'What did you hope for me? Have I fulfilled your expectations, or am I a disappointment?'

She should have been able to ask, but somehow it was impossible, so she helped herself to another jam tart, and began to talk about Rhodes, producing the presents she had brought back for them all, laughing and chattering as if there was no subdued ache in her heart at all. As if everything was fine, and she was the beloved elder daughter who had never been away.

Except of course it wasn't like that, and never would be again. Alix supposed the invisible barrier which had grown up was of her own making. She had underestimated the depth of her mother's hurt when she decided to go and work for Bianca. Underestimated it, because she didn't understand it.

Things might have been better when Debbie came home at teatime, but oddly they weren't. Debbie's greeting was perfunctory, and although she thanked Alix for her gift, her heart wasn't in it.

'Three weeks on Rhodes.' Her tone was frankly envious. 'The most Paul and I can hope for is a few days in Bournemouth, or somewhere.'

Alix glanced at the pretty, discontented face and made up her mind.

'Would you like a glamorous honeymoon as a wedding present?' she asked.

'No, thanks.' The swiftness of Debbie's response was almost insulting.

'Why not?' Alix enquired.

Debbie shrugged. 'We'll manage,' she said. 'I don't want to start my married life on your charity.'

Alix felt as if she had been pierced to the heart, but she managed to say equably, 'I'm sorry that you see it like that. I really didn't intend . . .'

'It doesn't matter what you intended,' Debbie cut

across her rudely. 'We're quite all right as we are. We don't need you playing Lady Bountiful.'

'That's quite enough, Debbie.' Margaret, who had been out of the room, had returned in time to hear the last part of the exchange. She went on, 'You'll have to excuse her, Alix. She's rather on edge these days.'

'Perhaps I'd better go.' Alix stood up, reaching for her bag. She was desperately afraid that she might burst into tears. Until she had left home, she and Debbie had shared a room, had confided in each other, giggled and occasionally quarrelled. Now they could be strangers.

'I'll see you out,' said Debbie.

'There's really no need.' Alix let a note of sarcasm enter her voice. 'This is still my home, and I've no intention of stealing anything on my way through the hall.'

'Alix!' her mother protested, smiling nervously. 'I'm sure Debbie didn't mean that.'

Alix gave her a quick kiss, aware of the tightness in her throat. 'Goodbye, love, and look after yourself. I—I'll telephone first next time.'

She walked through the hall without looking back, and shut the front door behind her. Then, feeling dazed, she made her way down the path to the gate. She was sure that Debbie was watching her from the front room window, but pride forbade that she should turn and confirm her certainty. It was raining lightly again, and she turned up the collar of her cream trench coat, and pushed her hands into her pockets as she hurried along towards the station.

What a total disaster of a day this had been! The grey skies as she flew in that morning had been an omen.

'I should have flown right out again,' she told herself with mordant humour.

Walking along, her head bent, she didn't see the figure approaching until she found herself in a mini-collision.

She said, 'I'm so sorry . . .' and broke off as a female voice exclaimed delightedly, 'Alix—Alix Coulter! How marvellous! Don't you remember me?'

Alix looked into the smiling face of Gemma Allan, an old school friend.

'Gemma—you're the last person I expected to see.'

'I can't think why. Didn't your mother tell you that Dave and I had bought the house on the corner? Didn't she give you my message?'

Alix shook her head bewilderedly. 'She must have forgotten. And of course I've been away—abroad.'

'That I can see.' Gemma whistled appreciatively. 'Is that an all-over tan, may one enquire? I'm brown too, of course, but with me it's rust.'

'Oh, Gemma!' To her horror, Alix heard her voice become choky. 'It's so great to see you.' To see a friendly face, she almost said.

'Hey,' Gemma took her arm, peering at her with concern, 'what's the matter? You're upset—what is it? Your mother?'

'Not really,' Alix shook her head, fighting back her tears. 'Oh, God, this is awful. I can't stand in the middle of the road bawling like a baby.'

'Then come and bawl in our house,' Gemma said soothingly. 'Dave won't be home for at least another hour.'

By the time they were settled in Gemma's small sitting room, Alix had managed to regain control of herself.

'I'm sorry to have behaved like an idiot,' she began.

'Think nothing of it,' Gemma said largely. 'Don't forget I'm used to it, having been at school with you. What's troubling you? You haven't had the sack from the dream job of yours?'

Alix smiled drearily. 'No, but I sometimes wonder whether I did the right thing in taking it in the first place.'

Gemma stared at her. 'Well, it has to be better than a lifetime of "Now this conveyance witnesseth as follows",' she said drily. 'Is it man trouble?'

'It is a man, and he is trouble, but not in the way that you mean,' Alix said ruefully. 'Look, the simplest thing is if I give you a quick run-down on "My Day so Far".'

Gemma sat and listened attentively, her sole comment being, 'Little bitch,' when Alix described Debbie's reaction to her offer of a honeymoon.

'She must be very unhappy,' Alix said slowly.

'She must be very jealous,' Gemma retorted.

'But she had no reason to be jealous of me,' Alix protested. 'She's always done exactly what she wanted, and now she's going to be married.'

Gemma looked at her pityingly. 'Look, love, Debbie would envy a dead man his coffin. Haven't you seen through her yet? She's probably as mad as fire that she wasn't offered your job.'

'But she couldn't have been. She hadn't even left school . . .'

'That's the reasonable point of view. Debbie wouldn't see it like that. She would see it as you getting a chance she'd been denied. Being married is the only other option open to her. I hope, for her fiancé's sake, that it works. Now, about this other business, why do you suppose Bianca doesn't want her biography written?'

Alix sighed. 'I wish I knew. She was all for the idea originally, when she thought someone was going to ghost it for her.'

'In other words a self-portrait by her greatest fan,' Gemma's voice was dry. 'Well, Liam Brant is no one's fan, so I suppose she can be allowed her misgivings.'

'Do you know him?' Alix stared at her.

'No, but I've read some of his books. Dave bought me the Kristen Wallace biog for my birthday, and what an eye-opener that was. Since then I've been borrowing his other stuff from the library.'

'Have you got any of them now?'

'I've one—an early one about Clive Percy, the conductor. He doesn't pull his punches, but he really gets inside the people he writes about. He makes you feel you know them.'

'Or at least you know what he wants you to know about them,' Alix said with some asperity. 'You can't really say he's objective.'

Gemma shrugged. 'Well, we won't argue about it. Have you read any of them?' And when Alix shook her head with a little grimace, 'Well, take the Percy one. It doesn't have to go back for a fortnight, and if you keep it longer than that, you pay the fine. Is it a deal?'

Alix laughed. 'Yes, it's a deal.' She stood up. 'Thank you for letting me talk it all out. I actually feel much better. Instead of an early night, I might just treat myself to dinner and a theatre.'

'I was going to offer you egg and chips with us, but your plan has far more going for it,' Gemma said cheerfully. 'But you will come to supper soon, won't you? Dave would love to meet you. I've mentioned you often. And now you've got my address and phone number, there's really no excuse . . .'

Alix felt infinitely happier as she left Waterloo, and hailed a taxi to take her into the West End. It had been marvellous to bump into Gemma like that. They had been so close at school, but afterwards it was only too easy to lose touch. She was ashamed to think that she hadn't even known that Gemma was married, let alone met her husband, and she couldn't help wondering why the family hadn't told her, because they must have known.

I could at least have sent a present, even if I couldn't have gone to the wedding, she thought wistfully.

Gemma had referred to her life with Bianca as a 'dream job', but suddenly Alix wasn't so sure. She'd begun to realise how totally and exclusively involved she was in her new life. Was it any wonder she was almost a stranger in her own home?

She would have to insist that Bianca gave her regular time off in future, so that she could set about rebuilding some of the relationships that had suffered in the past months—especially that with Debbie. She couldn't wholly accept Gemma's dismissal of Debbie's attitude as resentment and jealousy. She herself must be to blame in some way, and she could only be thankful that she had the opportunity to put things right before they went too far and there was a complete estrangement.

Working for Bianca had been allowed to take her over. She lived, dressed, snatched her meals, even took her holidays at Bianca's imperious behest. She smiled wryly as she recalled how Bianca had tossed the plane tickets and hotel reservation in Rhodes to her quite casually one day.

'Here you are, darling. You're looking pale and wan, and it depresses me.'

Alix could have protested—should have done, she told herself reflectively. She could afford holidays for herself. Heaven knew, she had enough money. Her living expenses were so few that she now had a healthy deposit account in the bank.

But she didn't argue, partly because Bianca liked to have her generous impulses received with due appreciation, and partly because she wanted to get away for a while anyway.

If she looked pale and strained, Bianca might well be experiencing guilt rather than depression, she decided cynically. And it would undoubtedly be convenient for her employer to have her out of the way for a few weeks, while the affair she was having with Peter Barnet burned itself out.

It wasn't the first time it had happened, of course. Peter was a journalist working for a show business column on one of the national dailies, and he had been invited to one of Bianca's cocktail parties. He was young, blond and undeniably attractive, and Alix had been attracted. She had enjoyed talking to him, and not been altogether surprised when he telephoned her and asked her to have dinner with him. She had seen him several times when Bianca had suggested, almost idly, that she might like to invite him to make up the numbers at a small dinner party she was giving.

Alix's impulse had been to refuse. She knew what would happen; she had seen it all before. It was as if Bianca could not bear to see any personable man paying attention to anyone other than herself. Other men who had dated Alix had either found themselves frozen out, or overwhelmed with a display of charm calculated to undermine any masculine defences.

Alix had not been in love with Peter, or with any of the others, but all the same it had not been pleasant to sit on one side of Bianca's gleaming dining table and watch Peter succumb without a struggle. He and Alix had talked and laughed and enjoyed each other's company, but he had never stared at her with that look of hot and glittering desire that he was turning on Bianca. Dinner ended, the other guests departed and Alix invented a headache to take her up to her room.

What happened after that was anyone's guess. And Alix didn't want to know. Nor, she found, did it help to tell herself that the ache in her heart was dented pride and no more. She was tired of having to face the fact of how easily Bianca could eclipse any charms she might have. It was hurtful to see someone she had liked apparently forget that she existed.

She knew the pattern, of course. Bianca's little flings were unvarying. There would be flowers delivered, and long intimate phone calls, often while Alix was in the room, with Bianca lying on her chaise-longue, the receiver cradled against her cheek.

Alix couldn't really be sorry that she was going to miss this particular episode in the long-running saga of Bianca's love life.

And she thought, 'I'd be frightened to let myself love someone in case she did the same thing to him. I might have loved Peter, for all she knew, but it made no difference. She still has to prove that she's irresistible.'

As she queued at the box office of the theatre of her choice, Alix found herself wondering without too much

curiosity what had happened to Peter. She could imagine, of course. One day, out of the blue, he would
have found that Miss Layton was no longer accepting
his calls. She wondered if he had accepted the situation
with dignity, or made a scene. Not that it would have
mattered. When it was over for Bianca, it was over, and
there were no reprieves.

The disappointments of the day were still with her
when she reached the box office window, to be told regretfully that all the seats had been sold, including the
few returned tickets. And there was no prospect of any
more cancellations.

Alix turned away ruefully. There were other theatres
and other plays, of course, but this was the one she had
set her heart on. She should have realised the necessity
to book. She stood in the street outside the theatre,
trying to decide what to do next. She would have dinner,
of course, and then back to the house, she supposed, for
an early night. Or she could always read the Clive Percy
book, she thought with a glance at the parcel in her
hand.

There was a small Italian restaurant just round the
corner and she would eat there, she decided, deliberately
removing from her mind the remembrance that Peter
had taken her there.

Even though it was comparatively early in the evening, the restaurant was quite busy, its tables mostly
occupied by couples. Alix was shown to a corner table,
given a menu and offered an aperitif. She ordered a
Cinzano and leaned back in her chair, a feeling of re-
laxation and contentment beginning to steal over her.
Perhaps she wouldn't have an early night after all. There
was a musical she wouldn't mind seeing—and there were
cinemas. She would ask the cheerful proprietor if he
had an evening paper and see what was on.

Aware that someone had stopped beside her table,
she looked up with a smile, expecting that her drink had
arrived.

Liam Brant said courteously, 'Good evening, Miss Coulter. We meet again.'

Alix felt the smile freeze into something like a grimace. Without stopping to think, she said hotly, 'You wouldn't be following me, by any chance?'

His brows lifted. 'You flatter yourself, secretary bird. As it happens, I often eat here. The food is good and the service is quick. I hope that reassures you.'

It wasn't particularly reassuring to know that she'd just made a fool of herself, so Alix remained silent, staring down at the checked gingham tablecloth.

'And what are you doing out of your gilded cage?' the infuriating voice went on.

'I was hoping to enjoy myself,' Alix said coolly.

'Until I showed up,' he supplied.

She shrugged. 'You said it—I didn't.'

'You didn't have to. Has no one ever told you that your face is the mirror to your thoughts?' To Alix's annoyance, he drew out the chair opposite and sat down.

Stiffening, she said, 'I don't remember inviting you to join me.'

'There's nothing the matter with your memory—you didn't,' he returned. To the waiter who had just brought Alix's Cinzano, he said, 'A whisky and water, please. And we'll both have lasagne.'

Alix's fingers curled like claws round her glass. In a voice almost molten with rage, she said, 'I did not intend to order lasagne.'

'Then you should. It's particularly good here. Or do you always play safe with steak or scampi wherever you happen to dine?'

'Of course not,' she began, then compressed her lips angrily. She was not going to be drawn into a discussion of her eating habits. 'What I'm trying to say is that I'm perfectly capable of making my own choice from the menu, and I'd prefer to eat alone.'

'Is it a preference you often indulge?'

She had expected him to leave, but he showed no signs of moving. And now the waiter was bringing his drink, a basket of freshly baked rolls, and a carafe of house wine. She could have screamed.

'Well, why don't you?' he said.

'Why don't I what?'

'Swear at me—throw your drink in my face—storm out. Whatever hostile fantasy you're harbouring. I told you that you were transparent. Why don't you follow the family tradition and go into films? You'd probably make your fortune.'

'Because I'm quite content as I am, thanks.' Alix made her face and voice impassive. Transparent, she thought, simmering inwardly.

'That's a dull thing to be at your age. And I don't believe you.' He lifted his glass. 'Here's to the other Alix Coulter, and may she soon stand up.'

'There is no other.' Alix did not respond to the toast, or drink from her own glass. She was afraid she might choke.

'Oh?' He gave her a long speculative look which covered the pinned-back hair, and the muted neutral colours of dress, trench coat and bag. 'Then the girl I glimpsed on the stairs today was someone else—or a mirage, was she?'

Alix had forgotten the glimpse he had caught of her. She felt the colour rise in her face, and knew angrily that he had noticed it too and was faintly amused by it.

She said between her teeth, 'Mr Brant, I came here for a quiet meal, not to be interviewed. I'm not interested in being copy for your next book any more than my—than Bianca is.'

He said softly, 'I've no intention of writing a book about you, darling. Your cumulative experience of life could undoubtedly be covered in a short article, probably for a parish magazine. My questions are prompted by a normal male curiosity about why an attractive young woman insists on dragging about the place like a facsimile of Little Orphan Annie. I assume it is deliberate.'

'I'm a working girl, Mr Brant, not some kind of starlet. Does that satisfy your curiosity?'

'It doesn't satisfy anything about me.' His eyes never left her face. 'You're a walking intrigue, Miss Coulter. I shall look forward to solving your particular mystery over the next few weeks. What was that wrongly buttoned dress—a Freudian slip?'

'I had to change in a hurry.' Alix heard a sudden breathless note creep into her voice. He was right about there being nothing the matter with her memory—she could remember the details of that little incident only too well.

'So did Cinderella when the clock struck midnight. Do you have some private timing device to tell you when the ball is over?'

'I really don't know what all the fuss is about,' Alix said with a hint of desperation. 'Just because I prefer to dress in a—in a businesslike way during working hours . . .'

'Another of these famous preferences of yours—you prefer to dress badly—you prefer to eat alone. Or are either of those choices, in fact, yours?'

'What do you mean?' Alix was stung. 'I don't dress badly. How dare you!'

'I dare quite easily. That dress you're wearing, for example—the style doesn't flatter your figure, and the colour does nothing for you at all.'

'Are you an expert on women's clothes as well as character assassination, Mr Brant?'

'I have a certain amount of expertise in a number of things,' he drawled with a sudden sideways grin, and she felt that betraying blush flood her cheeks again, as shaken as if his hand had brushed her skin, or his mouth touched hers . . .

The waiter bustled up with the dishes of lasagne, and she thought she had never been so glad to see anyone in her life. Not that she felt like eating. On the contrary, any appetite she had had was destroyed, although she had to admit that the smell of meat and spices emanating from the dish in front of her was a beguiling one.

'You're staring at it as if you think it might leap out of the dish and bite you instead.' Liam Brant sounded amused. 'I promise you it won't. Nor does it contain a secret drug which will put you in my power. Here,' he took the fork from her unresisting fingers, and scooped up a portion, offering it to her as if she had been a child, 'try it and see.'

She didn't want to take the food from him. She could see the couple at the next table exchanging indulgent glances.

She thought hysterically, 'They must think we're lovers. This is the sort of game lovers play—feeding each other with titbits at candlelit tables. I ought to tell them the truth—that I don't trust him, that I could even hate him. And yet at the same time that it would be easy—so easy to be in his power. And it wouldn't need secret drugs.'

She bent her head and ate the proffered forkful in silence.

'That wasn't so bad, was it?' His voice was still amused.

'No, you were right. The food here is delicious.' She sounded cool and composed, and she was proud of herself. 'Now, if I could have my fork, I did learn to feed myself as a child.'

'Ah,' he said. 'But what else have you learned since?'

Alix took another gulp of wine. How nice it must be to have an answer for everything, she thought sourly. No doubt when she was in bed later, trying to sleep, she would think of a dozen coruscating remarks with which she could have put him down permanently.

Oh, please let me wake up tomorrow and find the past twenty-four hours has all been a bad dream, she appealed silently to whatever benevolent deity might be listening, but without a great deal of hope.

She tried to make herself relax and enjoy her food, because if she obeyed her instinct and pushed her plate away almost untouched, he would probably guess that he was disturbing her and be amused.

'What did you eat the last time you came here?' he asked.

She put down her fork and stared at him. 'The last time?'

'With Peter Barnet,' he said. 'It was you.' A statement, not a question.

Alix moistened her lips with the tip of her tongue. 'I—I forget.'

'Clearly a memorable meal,' he said softly. 'Have you seen him lately?'

'As you appear to know my every move,' she said clearly, 'you tell me.'

'No, you haven't.' He leaned back in his chair, dark eyes watchful under hooded lids. 'Tell me, does Bianca Layton choose your clothes and hairstyle?'

'So that's it!' Alix gave a little artificial laugh. 'Not very clever, Mr Brant. What exactly are you probing for—some evidence of discontent? You won't find it. If you're trying to goad me into saying something about Bianca which you can interpret as disloyalty, then you're wasting your time. We have a very close relationship, and I'm grateful to her for all the opportunities I've had since I've been working for her. I'm sorry if my dress sense doesn't meet with your approval, but you sought my company, remember. I didn't seek yours.'

'Quite a speech,' he said drily. 'Didn't Shakespeare say something about protesting too much?'

'He may well have done,' she said. 'But I can assure you it doesn't apply in this case.'

He smiled lightly. 'As you wish. Now eat your food.'

'My appetite seems to have deserted me.'

'You're far too sensitive,' he remarked. 'Not a desirable attribute for anyone attached to the Layton menage, I would have thought.'

'If you disapprove of Bianca so strongly, why do you want to write about her? I thought biographers were supposed to be objective.'

'Who told you that?' he queried. 'I want to write about her because she's a great star, if not a great actress, and I'm interested in analysing the elements which come together to make such a being.'

'As you did with Kristen Wallace?'

'Right,' he agreed.

'Then you'll understand why I don't want you within a mile of Bianca.' She met his gaze fully, her own eyes blazing.

'The lamb leaps to protect the tigress,' he mocked. 'Calm down, Miss Coulter. There's no need for all this defensiveness, unless you already know that your idol has feet of clay. My researches may well reveal that under that highly lacquered exterior beats a heart of pure gold. I could always ask Peter Barnet's opinion.'

'Ask who you damned well like,' Alix said fiercely. 'But I'm telling you now, you'll get no co-operation from me, or from anyone else who works for Miss Layton. If you insist on writing this book, it will be an unauthorised biography, written without credibility, a rehash of everything that's been said before, with an additional helping of your own scurrilous brand of speculation, I have no doubt. Just don't expect any help.'

'What would you say,' he said softly, 'if I told you that you'd already helped more than you knew? Your lasagne must be stone cold by now. Would you like something else? Coffee, perhaps, and a brandy. You look as if you need it.'

'I don't want anything from you,' Alix said fiercely. She snatched up her handbag. 'If you'll tell me what my share of the bill is, I'll be going.'

'There's no hurry.' The dark face was smooth and

enigmatic as he watched her. 'The curtain doesn't go up for at least half an hour.'

'For once your Sherlock Holmes instinct has played you false,' she said between her teeth. 'I'm not going to the theatre. There are no seats left for the play I wanted to see.'

'There are, if you're talking about the show at the Galaxy. I was intending to go there myself tonight, but something's come up, so if you want one of my tickets you can have it.'

Alix stiffened. 'No, thank you.'

He smiled. 'Don't worry, I'm not trying to entrap you into spending the remainder of the evening with me.' He produced a slip of yellow paper from his wallet and put it on the table between them. 'It's a ticket for a play you want to see, that's all.'

'I want nothing from you,' snapped Alix on a little flare of temper.

'As you wish.' He shrugged slightly, then crumpled the ticket into a ball and tossed it into the empty ashtray. 'Have a pleasant evening.' He pushed back his chair and rose.

She said without looking at him, 'Goodbye, Mr Brant.' That was the second time she'd said that today, she thought wildly. Not that it had made any difference. And didn't people say that everything came in threes?

It made her skin crawl to think that she had sat in this very restaurant with Peter, being watched. She had laughed and talked and given herself away a hundred times, and all the time Liam Brant had been there taking note. And he knew why she was no longer seeing Peter too. That was quite obvious.

She was aware that the waiter was at her side, exclaiming in concern about her half-filled plate, asking her anxiously if the meal had been all right. She tried to assure him that everything had been fine, and that she had just not been hungry, refusing his offers of a dessert and coffee.

'If I could just have the bill, please.'

He looked mystified. 'The bill, *signorina*? But it has already been paid.' Mournfully he collected the plates and took them away, leaving Alix staring after him, her mouth set in fury.

Of course the bill had been paid, she thought angrily. Another barb in her flesh, a deliberate ploy to make her beholden to him even in a small way, like that damned theatre ticket.

How unfair it was that he should have a seat that he wasn't going to use for the play that she was dying to see. He must have seen her leaving the box office, she thought broodingly. Seen her and drawn his own conclusions.

She looked longingly at the little crumpled ball in the ashtray. What an awful waste it seemed. And as far as Liam Brant was concerned, that was the end of the matter. As soon as the table was cleared, the ticket would be thrown away, or so he thought. And it was only crumpled, not torn. If she was to use it, no one would be any the wiser.

Despising herself, she reached for the small yellow ball and smoothed the ticket out with fingers that shook a little. There was a war going on in her head, one part of her mind arguing fiercely that if she used the ticket, he would never know, and the other warning her that she should tear the ticket into tiny fragments rather than accept the slightest favour at his hands.

But what was the alternative? A quiet evening at home, unpacking and inevitably thinking about the problems the day had thrown up at her. It all seemed curiously unappealing.

She looked down at the ticket and told herself silently, 'He'll never know.'

The critics and theatregoers had been right; the cast and production thoroughly deserved the superlatives that had been heaped upon them.

In fact the only thing to mar Alix's contentment was

the second empty seat beside her. She had spent most of the first act in agony waiting for him to join her, preparing herself for the barbed comment, wondering whether it wouldn't be better to leave herself, before it happened.

But it didn't happen. Even after the interval the seat remained unoccupied, and she was able to relax and give herself over to the untrammelled enjoyment of the evening.

All the same, she couldn't help wondering exactly what had come up to prevent him seeing the play himself, and exactly who the second seat had been intended for. A woman undoubtedly, she thought, and attractive. His views on that were more than clear. An actress, maybe or a model, or perhaps a 'media person'. Someone glamorous, so that other people would look and look again, approving his choice and envying him.

She had a sudden disturbing inner image of his face, the cool dark eyes under the hooded lids, the thin high-bridged nose, and the sensuous curve of his lower lip. A man to whom women would matter. A man who would demand physical beauty, a physical response, she thought, remembering with a shiver the frank appraisal in his eyes, and the unwelcome brush of his fingers against her flesh.

That was something, she told herself, that she did not need to remember. She had managed to blot Peter Barnet and his defection out of her mind successfully. He wasn't even a dull ache any more, and she found it hard to recall anything about him except that he had been easy to talk to—but then he was a journalist, so he was probably professionally a good listener, she acknowledged wryly.

Yet she had never felt the same necessity to be on her guard with Peter as she did with Liam Brant.

When the final curtain call had been taken, and she rose and mingled with the laughing, chattering throng making their way towards the exits, Alix caught herself wondering whether she was the only person in the theatre to have watched the play alone. Everyone else around her seemed to be one of a couple, or part of a group, and she was aware of a lonely feeling deep inside.

Oh, come on, she addressed herself roughly, you've no need to feel sorry for yourself. You have a terrific life, and if this was the kind of outing you planned in advance, then you needn't have been alone.

She didn't usually feel so much like an outsider. It was the events of the day which had started her thoughts off in such a depressing train, she thought.

Outside the theatre, she realised that she was starving, but she determinedly turned her back on the Italian restaurant, preferring to walk a hundred yards or so to a much larger, brasher establishment which specialised in hamburgers and other forms of fast food.

The sort of place the Liam Brants of this world wouldn't be seen dead in, she decided with satisfaction, as she spooned pickles over the thick slice of grilled meat in her bun and bit into it appreciatively. She finished every crumb, and drank two cups of coffee for good measure.

It was raining again as she left the restaurant, and by some miracle she was able to hail a cruising taxi. My luck has changed, she thought, smiling as she leaned back in her seat.

The house was quiet as she let herself in at the front door, but Bianca was not in bed, because she could see a thread of light under the drawing-room door. For a moment she hesitated, then she walked across to the door and tapped lightly. It was understood that when she had been out, she always reported to Bianca on her return in case there were any urgent instructions. It wasn't unknown for Bianca to start dictating letters far into the night, or simply want to chat, or, when she was actually filming, have Alix hear her lines.

If there was no reply, then Alix would go discreetly up to her room, as she had done on many other occasions.

But she heard Bianca call, 'Come in,' so she pushed open the drawing-room door and walked into the room.

It was a cosy scene. The lamps were lit, the large cream-covered sofas had been drawn up round the fire, and a tray with a silver coffee pot, used cups and the remains of sandwiches stood discarded on the table.

Bianca, wearing one of the long velvet lounging gowns she often wore in the evenings, was lying curled up on one of the sofas.

She turned languidly and looked at Alix. 'Oh, there you are. Have you had a wonderful day?' She glanced smilingly at the man who sat on the other sofa. 'I think you've met Alix, my secretary, haven't you, darling?'

'Why, yes,' said Liam Brant.

CHAPTER THREE

ALIX felt as if she had been turned to stone. She stared at Liam Brant as if he was a mirage that would mercifully fade, but he clearly had no such intention. He moved, rose to his feet and smiled at her.

'An unexpected pleasure, Miss Coulter,' he said. 'Did you enjoy the play?'

She knew what he had done. He had deliberately used the ticket as bait in order to get her out of the way for the evening. He knew when he left the restaurant that she wouldn't be able to resist the temptation, and he had probably come straight here. But how on earth had he managed to be admitted to the house? How could he possibly be comfortably ensconced in Bianca's drawing room after everything she had said?

Unless, of course, she didn't know who he was.

She said, 'Unexpected, certainly, but a doubtful pleasure. Who let you in here?'

'Alix dear!' Bianca had also risen. She was smiling, but there was an underlying bite in her voice. 'I allow you a lot of leeway because of our relationship, but you really mustn't be rude to my guests.'

Alix exhaled sharply. 'You do realise who this is?'

'Of course,' Bianca shrugged. She turned to Liam, the smile widening. 'Alix is inclined to be a wee bit overprotective, so you must forgive her. She doesn't approve of anyone wanting to write the story of my life, and she's a little wary of the media in general at the moment.' The smile became intimate and a little rueful. 'Poor darling Alix is nursing a bruised heart, I'm afraid.'

She thought she would die of humiliation. She wanted to scream, 'It's not true! None of it's true,' but she remained silent.

Liam said with a trace of unholy laughter in his voice, 'Then her rather jaundiced attitude becomes altogether more understandable. As a matter of fact, Miss Coulter, it was you I called to see. I was on my way back to my flat when I realised I'd picked up a parcel of yours by mistake. I thought I'd better return it at once before you missed it and became worried.'

She recognised the package he had picked up from the sofa beside him. It was the book Gemma had lent her. One of his books.

She said, 'You really shouldn't have bothered, Mr Brant. It wasn't important.'

His mouth twisted mockingly. 'Perhaps the library might not agree with you. Anyway, Miss Layton and I encountered each other on the steps, and she was charming enough to agree to talk to me. I've been trying to convince her that I'm not as black as perhaps I've been painted.'

Oh, you've convinced her all right, Alix thought, seething. All that and more.

She knew the signs of old—the shaded lamps, the Harrises dismissed for the night to their own quarters, the clinging velvet gown—and the way Bianca was letting her eyes linger, meeting his gaze as if they were the only two people in the room, resting with unspoken appreciation on the width of his shoulders beneath the expensive wool jacket, the way his close-fitting pants clung to his hips.

It wasn't for real, of course, Alix thought cynically. Not on a first encounter. Bianca was just gently indicating the possibilities—making sure that he would return, a fly to her honeytrap.

He wasn't dazzled, as Peter had been, but then he was older than Peter—mid-thirties, she supposed—and infinitely more sophisticated.

If he decided to accept Bianca's delicately proffered invitation then it would be on his own terms, and she wondered if Bianca realised this.

And why should she care, anyway? she thought with a rush of irritation. Bianca was old enough and certainly experienced enough to look after herself. While she, Alix, wasn't experienced at all, which made her concern totally laughable.

She took the book from Liam Brant, thanking him coolly through compressed lips. It was galling to realise from his remark about the library that he knew exactly what the package contained, and was amused by it. He must have picked it up as he was leaving the table simply to provide himself with an excuse for calling back at the house.

It would have served him right, she thought savagely, if I'd been here after all, and answered the door, and put an end to all his wheeling and dealing. But of course, I wasn't here, and he knew that I wouldn't be. Clever Mr Brant. First create your opportunity, then exploit it to the full.

And now he was leaving, taking Bianca's hand with charming deference, and lifting her fingers lightly to his lips, while his eyes lingered on her mouth with unmistakable significance.

'Alix will show you out,' Bianca was saying. 'You two have simply got to be friends. Goodnight, Liam. *A bientôt.*'

Her smile seemed to indicate both regret and a promise, calculated to a nicety. It didn't really matter whether she was playing to the camera or a man, Alix thought wearily. She applied the same art and dedication to either situation.

She led the way out of the drawing room in silence and walked across the hall to the front door.

He said softly, 'Well, secretary bird, why don't you call me some of the unladylike names which are no doubt hovering on your extremely ladylike lips?'

'Situations change, Mr Brant, and I have to change with them.' She kept her voice even. 'This morning you were *persona non grata*. Tonight you're the flavour of the month. Congratulations.'

'Everybody's choice but yours, poor darling Alix.' He put out a hand and lifted her chin, forcing her to look at him. 'As we seem destined to spend a considerable amount of time around each other, shall we declare a truce? There's little point in waging a war you can't win, particularly when the general has deserted you.'

'Please don't celebrate your victory too soon,' she said icily. 'It may not be a lasting one. Don't run away with the idea that Bianca is a pushover, because she isn't.'

'She's certainly right about your over-protectiveness,' he said drily. 'As a matter of fact it's none of your business. Your beautiful relative and I are both consenting adults and free to come to whatever arrangement seems best to us.'

'You believe in being frank.' Alix was annoyed to feel the colour rising in her cheeks.

'And you don't? You couldn't have been more disapproving if you'd caught us in bed together.'

'Then I must apologise. As you say, it's none of my business.' Her voice sounded colourless. 'Perhaps you'd excuse me now. It's been a long day.'

'The first of many, I suspect,' he said coolly. 'Goodnight, poor darling Alix. Sleep well.'

She closed the door behind him, locked it, fastened the bolts, and attached the chain, moving like an automaton.

When she got up to her room, she was shivering. She took off the despised trench coat and let it drop to the floor. Then she took a long, level look at herself in the mirror. There she was—'poor darling Alix', someone to be pitied in an amused way, then shrugged aside and disregarded. Muted, dull and drab, in her very ordinary dress.

She unfastened her hair and shook it loose around her shoulders. Better, but not much, she thought. The dress was to blame, of course. Basically, it was shapeless—or at least its shape didn't conform to hers in the ways which mattered. The colour too was wrong for her skin tone.

She began to take it off, tugging so sharply at the buttons that at last one of them tore away. She went on staring at herself, aware of an odd satisfaction. She slipped her finger experimentally into the rent in the material and widened it, then pulled with both hands. The bodice split irrevocably, down to the waistline, and beyond.

Alix said grimly, 'So that's the end of you.' She stepped out of the remains, and kicked them away from her. She gave a sudden giggle, then clapped her hands over her mouth.

What was happening to her? she asked almost despairingly. What on earth was she doing, standing around in her bra and half-slip laughing like an idiot because she'd just torn an expensive dress almost to shreds?

And why had she done such a crazy thing? Because a man she didn't even like had looked at her and found her lacking in sex appeal, had criticised her appearance.

'Oh God,' she whispered, her mouth trembling. Only twenty-four hours ago she had been on her way home from Rhodes, rested, relaxed and prepared to take up her life again on the terms offered. Now there seemed endless confusion within her.

She bent and picked up the torn dress, throwing it across the bed. Then once again she looked at herself in the mirror, examining herself half fearfully as if she had undergone some sea change.

The curtains were drawn across the window, and only one lamp—a cream-shaded one by the side of the bed—was lit. She stood in the shadows, her dark hair tangling on her shoulders, the crisp, lacey lines of the half-cup bra emphasising the curve of her small breasts.

As if she was a puppet at the mercy of some unknown

force manipulating the strings, she felt herself turn
slightly, lifting her chin. Saw her lips curve and part,
her eyes gleam with promise through her lowered lashes.
Saw a total reflection of the image Bianca had projected
only minutes before, all woman, all sensuous provocation. It was the look that had become her trademark.
The look which made strong men buckle at the knees
and cameras melt.

It was one of the clips they often played on the movie
programmes—ranking with Lauren Bacall's famous
'You know how to whistle, don't you, Steve?' It had
been imitated a hundred times with differing degrees of
success.

And just for a moment—one tiny second out of the
whirl of time—Alix hadn't recognised herself. For a
moment she had looked into the mirror and seen
Bianca.

She stepped back quickly, pushing her hair back from
her face, picking up her flowered cotton housecoat and
putting it on, tying the sash tight, with quick, nervous
gestures. Dull but familiar, she thought. She was herself
again, Alix, the efficient, obedient secretary, and that
dark, unsuspected stranger who had surfaced just then
could go back to whatever fantasy realm she inhabited,
and stop rehearsing for a role she would never be called
on to play.

She turned away from the mirror, moving towards
the bed, then stopped suddenly. The confusion within
her was fading, leaving a terrible aching clarity in its
place. Why—now of all times—did she feel like this?

But she knew why. She thought of Bianca alone with
Liam Brant and the inner pain gripped her again like a
clenched fist.

She said aloud, 'No,' and again, 'Oh, no!' She must
be going crazy. She'd been attracted before to men—of
course she had. But instinct told her that what she felt
now went deeper by far than mere attraction. She was
experiencing desire for the first time in her life. Desire

for a man whose sole interest in her had been as a stepping stone by which he might reach Bianca. A man whom Bianca had already marked down as her own.

Alix sank down on the edge of the bed with a little groan. As the shadows seemed to close in around her, she thought, 'What am I going to do?'

She hadn't slept, but her Greek tan, coupled with the careful application of make-up, disguised the telltale marks. Now as she made her way along the corridor to Bianca's room, she was mentally rehearsing what she had to say.

She had dressed to give herself courage in some of her holiday gear, a short-sleeved, scoop-necked green top, and a matching button-through skirt. She had brushed her dark hair back from her face, but left it loose.

Bianca's sitting room and bedroom were both deserted, as they usually were at that time of the morning. Alix walked across the bedroom to the door in the corner, half hidden by a looped curtain of rose silk.

The room beyond was where Bianca got down to the real business of making herself ready for the day ahead. It had once been an ordinary dressing room, but imagination and unlimited resources had transformed it into something between a gymnasium and a beauty parlour. There was a sauna with an adjacent shower cubicle tiled in aquamarine, while an archway led into a bathroom with a circular sunken bath in the middle. There were exercise machines, and a multitude of beauty aids lined up on the wall-length vanitory unit, topped by carefully lit mirrors.

In the middle of all this was a high couch, and here Bianca lay discreetly covered by towels while Monty in a crisp white overall gave her her morning massage.

She looked up at Alix and smiled lazily. 'Good morning, sweetie.' Then as her eyes fell on the single envelope in Alix's hand. 'My God, surely that isn't all the mail?'

'I haven't been down to the office yet,' Alix returned.

'I see.' The smile faded as Bianca studied her for a moment, her eyes taking in the casual clothes, the smooth tan of her bare legs. 'You seem to have decided to carry on with your holiday for a few days.'

'You could say that,' Alix said calmly. 'Actually I'm here to hand in my notice. I'd like to leave as soon as possible.'

There was an electric silence. Monty's busy hands stopped suddenly and Bianca levered herself upwards, staring at Alix increduously.

'This is far too early in the morning for jokes, Alix. What's the matter with you?'

'I'm not joking.' Alix placed the envelope down on the vanitory unit. 'I've put it in writing.'

'I don't care whether you've put it in Cyrillic script,' Bianca snapped. Her face was flushed. 'Don't be such a fool! You can't possibly want to leave. You've no reason—no reason at all.'

Alix looked at her steadily. 'None?'

Bianca had the grace to look faintly guilty. 'Are you upset about last night? You've no need to be. I had to say what I did. I thought you'd understand.'

'You've always understood before' hovered unspoken in the air between them. And so she had. Part of her job had been to allow herself to be used in whatever ploy Bianca was engaged in. But she wasn't the same person any more.

She shrugged. 'It's only partly that. The fact is I can't come to terms with the fact that you've changed your mind over the book again. I think it's a bad move on your part, and that Liam Brant is a dangerous man. I can't guarantee the kind of co-operation over the project that you'd expect, so it's best if I leave.'

'That's a rather extreme reaction,' Bianca said,

sounding a little amused. 'But there's no need to be a martyr. There isn't going to be any book—at least, there won't be for some time to come. We're going to Italy.'

She relaxed again, pillowing her turban-swathed head on her folded arms, and Monty returned to her task, the soothing firmness of her hands at variance with the set grimness of her mouth.

'Since when have we been going to Italy?' Alix felt utterly bewildered.

'Since yesterday lunchtime.' Bianca's smile reflected the satisfaction of the cat who hasn't even had to steal the cream but has been offered it on a saucer. 'I've had an invitation from darling Carlo to go and stay with him in his villa outside Rome.' Her smile widened. 'And you know what that means—that I'm definitely going to play Francesca. My God, won't there be some wailing and gnashing of teeth when the word gets out!'

There probably would be at that, Alix thought. The role of Francesca was one of the cinema plums of the year, and the search for the right actress to play the part had been a publicity man's dream. Bianca had known for some time that she was on an unofficial short list, and she had been expecting the director Carlo Veronese to visit London in the next few weeks to make his decision.

'Leon told me at lunch that he wants to discuss the script with me,' Bianca said smugly. 'He feels that if we go and stay at the villa, it will provide a more relaxed atmosphere.' She stretched luxuriously. 'God, do I feel good this morning!'

'Keep still, then,' Monty said dourly. 'That's if you want to look good as well.'

Bianca laughed. 'Old grouch!'

Her good humour revealed how deeply the invitation from Carlo Veronese had reassured her, Alix thought. It had been by no means certain that she would get the part of Francesca. A number of other actresses had been under consideration, most of them a great deal younger than Bianca, but without her experience in films. Yet there would have to come a time when experience no longer counted, when the public, however devoted, would react with scepticism to an actress who had been a star for so many years attempting to play a young girl.

Alix knew that Seb had been worried about this for some time, although he had never dared tackle Bianca directly on the subject.

'Looking ageless—which admittedly she does—simply isn't enough any more. You have to *be* young these days, not merely look it. The people who still go to the cinema are more selective than they used to be—and more cynical,' he had said worriedly only a few months before when the possibility that Bianca might play Francesca had first been mooted.

Alix could understand why Bianca coveted the role. It was a reversion to the kind of dramatic, passionate woman's film that Bette Davis and Joan Crawford had made so successful, the novel from which it had been adapted having shot to the top of the bestsellers' list in spite of the sneers of the critics.

It was unashamed escapism, she supposed, because it was set among the wealthy and powerful, yet its theme was the exploitation of women, and the bitter ending had a certain harsh realism. It was a powerful story which would undoubtedly adapt well to strong visual terms.

Nor was there any doubt that Francesca was a young woman's role, taking the character as it did from naïve girlhood to the strength and disillusion of the early thirties. It was the kind of part that was every actress's dream. And Carlo Veronese was one of those directors whom every actress wanted to work for.

His films usually enjoyed a high degree of success, artistically as well as at the box office. Yet he had a predilection for discovering young and unknown actresses, rather than using established stars, and Bianca could regard the fact that his choice had fallen on her for Francesca as a feather in her cap.

With an effort Alix switched her attention back to what Bianca was saying. Normally she would have made the travel arrangements for the journey, but this was being done by Leon's office as he would be accompanying them.

'You can tell the Harrises that they can have a vacation,' Bianca said carelessly. 'I'll close the house up for a while, because after Italy we'll be going on to America. All the location work will be done there.'

Alix heard her with some dismay. She wasn't sure she wanted to be away from England for such a long time. She needed a period of adjustment to get back on terms with her family again. If it was her frequent absences which had made her relationship with them so strained, then another lengthy time abroad wasn't going to help.

Carefully she asked, 'Are you sure you need me to go with you?'

Bianca lifted her head sharply, her satisfied smile disappearing as if it had been wiped from her face. 'Of course I do. What the hell's the matter with you, girl? Just because we're related it doesn't mean that you can treat your work lightly. You're my secretary, in case it had slipped your mind. There'll be plenty for you to do.'

Alix saw a grim smile flicker briefly over Monty's features as she adjusted the towels which covered Bianca and began to massage her neck with practised, skilful fingers.

She doesn't just resent me, she thought unhappily. She really enjoys hearing me taken to task. Surely she knows by now that Bianca makes no real allowances for the fact that we're related. She has nothing to fear from me. She has a special relationship with Bianca which no outside intervention can damage, and she must know that.

She said quietly, 'I'm sorry, Bianca. I'll go and deal with the mail.' She hesitated. 'If—if Mr Brant should telephone, what do you want me to say to him?'

'Just put him through to me.' Bianca began to smile again, her expression openly sensuous. 'I'll talk to him.'

Alix guessed that the Italian trip would be a well-kept secret from Liam Brant until Bianca chose to reveal it. And undoubtedly she would have her own way of making up to him for his disappointment over the commission, she thought detachedly. What a fool she had been to imagine for one moment that Bianca needed her protection! She had her own methods of dealing with any threats that came along. Her earlier panic when she had ordered Alix to get rid of Liam Brant seemed to have been altogether forgotten. Clearly she found him less formidable in the flesh than he was by reputation, but was she right in this?

Alix shrugged mentally as she made her way downstairs to her office. The matter was out of her hands anyway, and she ought to be thankful for it. Her miserable, restless night had alarmed her. It was so out of character. A disturbing influence like Liam Brant was the last thing she needed in her life, particularly when it was so obvious that he was to be Bianca's perquisite. She had come very close to making an utter fool of herself, and although she couldn't welcome this trip to Italy, at least it might help to restore her normal equilibrium.

The next ten days seemed to fly past. Alix determinedly kept herself as busy as possible, and took care to be out of the way if she even suspected that Liam Brant was to be a visitor at the house. Bianca rarely mentioned him, but she too had her preoccupations. She was bored with her current wardrobe, and was busy amassing a pile of new clothes in which she was to impress Carlo Veronese. She was also being almost neurotic over her weight and appearance, and actually took off for a few days at an expensive health farm.

Monty was not pleased by this, and as usual when Bianca had done something she disapproved of, came as close to unbending to Alix as she was ever likely to.

'She doesn't need to lose as much as an ounce,' she said, thin-lipped. 'She'll make herself ill if she's not careful, and then where will we all be?'

She glared at Alix as if the health farm had been her idea.

Alix smiled temperately. 'Perhaps she's being a bit obsessive at the moment, but it's easy to understand why. This Francesca thing means such a hell of a lot to her.'

'I know that.' Monty's brow was creased with sudden anxiety. 'Only too well I know it! She wants to be a girl again.' She stopped suddenly as if she was aware of saying too much, and that Alix was the enemy within the gate.

As she still seemed to be in her own home. She had made a point of visiting her family several times, trying not to be hurt at the coolness of the welcome she received. She and her father had never been particularly close, as she had often realised, so she could not complain of any change in his attitude, but she was increasingly concerned about her mother. Margaret Coulter looked more tired each time she went, and seemed to be retreating into some inner kingdom where no one could follow. And Debbie's hostility hadn't abated one jot, she discovered to her dismay. To be sure, her sister was immersed in the details for her wedding, and had little time to spare for discussion about anything else, but there had been a time when Debbie would have shared her plans and excitement with her sister. As it was, Alix knew she was being deliberately excluded.

It was upsetting to realise that she was far more welcome at Gemma's than she was in her own home. She had now met Gemma's husband, who was large, genial and easygoing, and found herself envying the evident satisfaction they derived from their relationship.

She confided to Gemma her growing concern about her mother.

'I asked her if she'd thought of seeing a doctor, and she almost bit my head off,' she said ruefully. 'She doesn't seem to have any energy, and that isn't like her. I tried to drop a hint to Debbie, but she implied I was making a fuss about nothing, and that it wasn't really my business anyway. I don't know what to do.'

'You can't really do anything.' Gemma added washing up liquid to a sinkful of hot water, and swished it into lather. 'You can't force her to see a doctor if she doesn't want to, and there may be nothing the matter with her. Debbie's wedding might be making her a bit uptight. Had you thought of that?'

'You're probably right, but I just feel so—helpless, I suppose.' Alix could not suppress a pang as she mentally contrasted Margaret's rather grey-looking skin and shadowed eyes with Bianca's radiant appearance, fresh from her health farm.

She'd tried to suggest gently to her mother that a week or two in a similar establishment would be of benefit to her, but Margaret had dismissed the idea out of hand.

'No doubt it's kindly meant, but I have no inclination to go to a place like that, or time to waste either,' she had said shortly, and Alix had been made to feel tactless for having mentioned it.

'Do you want me to keep an eye on her while you're away?' Gemma rinsed glasses under the tap and put them on the draining board.

'I'd be so grateful.' Alix's eyes shone. 'But it's difficult. I don't really know where I'll be, or how you can get in touch with me.'

'I don't for one moment suppose I shall need to,' Gemma pointed out good-temperedly. 'I'm just trying to put your mind at rest, so that you can enjoy Italy.'

Alix sighed. 'I keep telling you, I'm not going there to enjoy myself. I'm going to work. Bianca expects her pound of flesh, whatever the setting.'

'All the same, you wouldn't swap with me,' Gemma grinned.

'Who says?' Alix retorted instantly, but in her heart she knew that Gemma was right. The girl she had been might once have been contented with the small semi-detached house, the amiable husband dozing in front of the television, but no longer.

She wasn't even sure about marriage any more. In the circles in which she now moved it seemed little more than a transitory experience. When she had first joined Bianca's ménage, her aunt was still married to Lester Marchant, and apparently happy, yet little more than a year later they had separated, and divorce—Bianca's fourth—had soon followed.

'Marriage is like a disease,' Bianca had once said petulantly. 'Thank God there's a cure.'

She had shown no signs of becoming involved in another serious relationship since Lester's departure, however. But there had been numerous casual affairs. Bianca was not a woman who could be without a man for very long.

And Alix wondered if it was not significant that the lovers she had chosen since this last divorce were not solid older men like Lester, but usually very much her junior. It was as if Bianca was constantly seeking reassurance that she was still beautiful, still desirable in spite of the passage of the years no one was even allowed to mention.

And perhaps it was watching Bianca, absorbing her example, which had made Alix herself so wary in her relationships, at least until recently.

Try as she might, there were times—in dreams, and in unguarded waking moments—when Liam Brant's dark cool mockery returned to haunt her. No amount of shame or self-admonition was sufficient, it seemed, to wipe his image totally from her mind, and this realisation bewildered and tormented her.

Gemma asked, 'What on earth are you thinking about? You looked positively haunted for a moment!'

Alix made herself smile. 'I suppose I am—by the thought of everything that has to be got through before this trip. Leon's office may be making all the arrangements for the journey, but there are still a hundred and one things Bianca wants me to do, and the fact that she changes her mind constantly about each of them doesn't make life any easier.'

She chattered on, making Bianca's vagaries sound amusing, deliberately shutting out of her mind the difficulties that her employer constantly seemed to create, the barbed remarks which so often seemed to enter her conversations with Alix these days.

Alix supposed she herself was partly to blame because she had disregarded Bianca's instructions about her appearance, and it was this subject at which most of Bianca's gibes were aimed.

Not that she'd gone overboard, she thought ruefully, but she'd had her hair cut so that it could no longer be screwed back into that frankly unbecoming chignon. Now it swung dark and glossy as a raven's wing, curving towards her jawline, accentuating her high cheekbones, and the delicate hollows of her throat. She wasn't a beauty and never would be in Bianca's terms, but she had her own attractions and could see no valid reason to conceal them any longer.

Bianca had been so angry at first that Alix had quite expected her attempt to hand in her notice would be reciprocated. In fact the anger seemed totally out of proportion to the offence—but then so much of Bianca's behaviour was irrational, Alix reminded herself.

She had encountered unexpected sympathy from Monty, who had said gruffly, 'Leave her to me. I'll settle her down,' and had apparently done so, because the next time Alix had ventured into Bianca's presence the hectic flush had died out of her cheeks, and the stormy light in her eyes had been stilled.

Afterwards Alix had wondered if the anger might not have been easier to deal with than what followed—the smiling ridicule, the spiteful remarks cloaked in a smile like a wasp's sting in honey. She had smarted for hours at the way Bianca's eyes sometimes slid over her in half-pitying amusement.

She flayed herself with the thought that perhaps Liam Brant had told Bianca what he'd said, his criticisms of her appearance, and this was why Bianca watched her in that way. And yet if that had been the case she knew Bianca well enough by now to know that she couldn't have resisted the temptation to mention it, to lay the lash gently but surely along what was already an open wound.

Alix felt herself shiver at the thought. She had been incredibly naïve when she first came to work for Bianca, but over the years she had developed what she thought was a protective shell, a self-sufficiency which enabled her to tolerate Monty's resentment and Bianca's swift and not always kind changes of mood.

Up to a few weeks ago she had known a kind of security, until a man with a lean, dark face and cool scornful eyes had made her realise that her shell was no protection after all, that in reality she was still as vulnerable as a child. It was not a comforting realisation. She also had to face the fact that no matter how determinedly she might put all thought of Liam Brant out of her mind, he was not so easily disposed of. And every time she thought of him, her hands and body grew cold, and all her blood seemed to concentrate in some weird way in her face in a burning flush. It was a reaction she couldn't explain, because in her heart she knew she didn't want to consider the implications of such an explanation.

At least the Italian trip would give her something else to think about, she told herself, and wished she could have felt more reassured.

The flight got off to a hectic start. The Press, duly primed by Seb, were out in force. Alix supposed by this time she should be used to the questions, the flashing bulbs which usually attended Bianca's arrivals and departures at the world's international airports. Bianca Layton was news—and the fact that she had accepted an invitation to stay at Carlo Veronese's villa was hot news, although the statement Seb had prepared was playing the whole thing very cool. It said simply that Bianca was flying to Italy for a much needed holiday, and dismissed all speculation about the role of Francesca as unfounded and premature.

The statement hadn't pleased Bianca very much. She felt the triumph was hers and wished to savour it, but at last she reluctantly agreed it might be better to delay any announcement until the contract was signed, and that being so she played the part Seb had assigned to her for all she was worth.

She looked amazingly beautiful, Alix thought detachedly. Nor was it a question of bone structure and expert therapy. The appearance of a camera—any camera—effected a kind of alchemy. She seemed illuminated from within in some mysterious way. And today she was all charm and graciousness too, without a hint of the petulance which had sometimes soured her relations with the Press. It was an enchanting performance, and Alix, standing the usual discreet distance away with Monty, silently applauded.

The impromptu press conference was just beginning to break up when one journalist said, 'What's going to happen about the authorised biography of you, Miss Layton? I understand preliminary work has already started.'

Bianca's smile was radiant. She said, 'I think that's

also a little premature. Anything of that nature will have to be postponed indefinitely, of course. I shall be far too busy in the coming months, I'm afraid.'

And that was it, Alix thought, fascinated. Another problem solved, another cloud banished from her particular sky with a wave of the hand. Liam Brant had been relegated to the unimportant with a few casual words. She must be totally sure, totally secure in her power over him. She must have him eating out of her hand.

Their flight was being called, and Bianca was on her way, posing for last pictures, and calling smiling farewells to the columnists she knew by name. Alix noticed that Peter was not among them. He was probably licking his wounds somewhere, she thought, and could even feel sorry for him.

No one gave Monty and herself even a second glance as they followed Bianca at the same discreet distance to the aircraft.

The separation continued on the plane. Bianca and Leon were ensconced in the first class cabin, while Alix found herself in an adjoining seat to Monty in the second class accommodation.

She was thankful that it wasn't a long flight. She'd found herself in the same situation on several of the Transatlantic crossings, and Monty had hardly spoken a word to her. This time she was prepared; she had brought a book to read in her hand luggage. As she unfastened her seat belt and bent forward to retrieve it, she was suddenly aware that Monty was leaning back in her seat, her eyes closed, and her hands rigidly gripping the arm rests. She was alarmingly pale.

Alix asked, concerned, 'What is it? Are you feeling ill?'

After a long moment Monty's eyelids flickered, and she gave something approaching a wan smile.

She said, 'No, not ill. It—it just doesn't get any better, that's all. And this time for some reason it's a great deal worse.'

Alix stared at her in bewilderment. She said, 'Do you mean—are you scared of flying?'

It seemed impossible. Monty had been with Bianca for so many years. She was a seasoned traveller if ever there was one.

She was beginning to lose some of that awful rigidity and a little colour was creeping back into her face as she said with some of her old crispness, 'Ridiculous, I know, but I've never been able to help it. I usually take tablets, but I found this morning that I'd run out, and there wasn't time to get any more. They're on prescription, you see . . .' Her voice trailed away with a little uncertainty, and she turned her head and looked at Alix. She said, 'You won't tell her? She doesn't know—she's never known. She—she wouldn't like it.'

That was quite true, Alix thought. Monty was Bianca's stalwart. No sign of weakness would be tolerated, and Monty knew it. Knew that one day Bianca might look at her and realise that she was getting old. And when that happened all those devoted years, Monty's care and expertise, would count for very little.

She remembered Lester Marchant saying, 'She uses people until they've nothing left that she wants, then she discards them. Well, she's not using me up.'

He'd been angry, she remembered, and bitter, but there'd been hurt as well. She had only seen him once more. He had come into the office to say goodbye, and he'd kissed her cheek and said, 'Don't let her use you, Alix.'

She hadn't really understood what he meant then, because after all she was Bianca's secretary, and there to be used. It was what she was paid for. But gradually and painfully she had begun to see what he was getting at.

She said warmly, 'Of course I won't say anything. I don't know how you've managed to pretend all this time. I don't think I could be as brave as that.'

Monty's voice was tart. 'It's got nothing to do with bravery. It's self-preservation, and you know it. You're not a complete fool.' She paused and then said heavily, 'You're a good child in many ways. I don't think I've always been altogether fair to you. I never wanted you to work for her. I've never made any secret of it, and I blamed *him* for encouraging her. I told her it was a mistake, but she wouldn't listen.'

Alix listened in a kind of amazement. Monty had never spoken to her with such frankness before.

'But why?' she asked. 'I don't understand. Did you think I'd presume on our relationship?' She had to smile as she said it. The very idea of Bianca allowing anyone, even her own flesh and blood, to presume in any way was ridiculous.

But Monty did not join in her amusement. She said abruptly, 'I had my reasons. But it's turned out better than I thought—I'll admit that.'

And what an admission! Alix thought, startled. But she welcomed it if it meant that she and Monty would be on easier terms from now on. She wasn't wholly optimistic, of course. Monty might regret this unbending when she was safely down on the ground again.

She still looked pale and tense and when the stewardess came round to take orders for drinks, Alix ordered a brandy for her, as well as a gin and tonic for herself.

In the other cabin, Bianca would be drinking champagne with Leon, she supposed ironically. Bianca rarely drank spirits; she considered them ageing.

Monty swallowed her brandy with unusual obedience, and then seemed to doze for a while. Alix sipped her drink more slowly and watched the changing patterns of the clouds beneath the aircraft. Flying had never bothered her. It was just one of those things. At first she had even found it exciting, but it had soon dwindled into the ordinary—a part of life to be got through like everything else, but never to be dreaded as apparently poor Monty had always done.

Her mouth twisted ironically. Little did she think

when she got up that morning that she would be referring to the steel-backed, eagle-eyed Miss Montgomery
as 'poor Monty', even in thought. And it could only
ever be in thought. Monty's new-found tolerance of her
would vanish like morning mist if she suspected for a
moment that Alix pitied her.

Monty woke, and the stewardesses came round
serving lunch. They exchanged a few desultory remarks over the meal, and Monty seemed amiable
enough for Alix to ask her something she had often
wondered about.

'How did you meet Bianca in the first place?'

'Something like a reminiscent smile touched Monty's
lips. 'We were in rep together. Oh, yes,' she went on,
meeting Alix's surprised look. 'I was much older, and
playing character parts, and she was just beginning to
get juvenile leads. She was good, but I never thought
the stage was the right medium for her. I always thought
films—or television.'

Alix was thoroughly bewildered. Monty as a
character actress was something which had never
occurred to her.

'But if you were in the theatre, how did you come to
learn massage and all the other things?'

'I had a fall, a bad one, which needed extensive treatment. At one time it seemed likely I was going to have a
limp, which meant my stage career was probably at an
end, so I had to look for something else to do. Massage
had been part of my treatment, and I became interested
in it. I decided to take a course, and beauty therapy was
part of it. I'd lost touch with Bianca after she left the
company, but I met her by chance one day in Harrods.
We had tea together, and she asked me what I was
doing.' She gave a half-shrug. 'Next thing was that she
offered me a job, and I've been with her ever since—
over twenty years.'

Another side of Bianca, Alix thought, surprised, extending a helping hand to an old friend. That kind of

loyalty didn't seem particularly characteristic of her aunt. After all, she had never displayed it towards her own family. Perhaps Lester Marchant's view was the true one—that Bianca had seen in Monty someone who could be useful to her, and it went no deeper than that.

She glanced at Monty and saw that she was staring straight in front of her with a rather brooding expression on her face. Perhaps the same thought had occurred to her.

To change the subject she said, 'I wonder what the villa will be like?'

Monty produced something like a sniff. 'Opulent, I expect.' She paused. 'And very warm.'

Alix laughed. 'Perhaps I shall be able to work on my tan.'

Monty gave her a considering look. 'You don't want to get too brown. It won't do your skin any good in later life.'

Alix said cheerfully, 'Oh, I don't really need to bother about things like that.'

'You should always bother about your appearance,' Monty said flatly. 'I thought from the look of you that you were beginning to take a real interest at last.'

Alix put up a hand and touched the silken fall of her hair. She said ruefully, 'I'm afraid Bianca isn't very pleased with me still.'

Monty shrugged. 'There's no reason why she should be. After all, you've reminded her of something she won't want to remember.'

'What's that?' Alix asked.

'What she looked like when she was a girl,' Monty said drily. 'Don't you remember the photographs she was going through—to illustrate the book?'

'I never really saw them. I went on holiday, and when I came back she'd changed her mind about the biography.' She stopped, because the mention of it had brought Liam Brant back into her mind again, and she was conscious of that deep fierce ache again. She noticed that the warning lights about smoking and seat-belts had come on again, and a voice was telling the passengers that they would be landing at Rome airport shortly. She bent her head and concentrated on her seat-belt, knowing that Monty would be doing the same and would not be able to watch her too closely.

Trying to make her voice casual, she said, 'Did Mr Brant mind very much—about the book? He—he seemed very set on it, I thought.'

'Heaven knows what he'll think.' Monty was clearly steeling herself for the descent, and disinclined for conversation.

Alix stared at her. 'Doesn't he know—that Bianca's going to Italy, I mean?'

'She did telephone him,' Monty said grudgingly. 'But there was no answer, and she wasn't pleased. She may have phoned again, but I doubt it. I think she was expecting him to be in touch with her. He'll know soon enough when he sees tomorrow's papers.'

She closed her eyes determinedly and leaned back in her seat with a deepening look of apprehension.

Alix felt apprehensive too, but it had nothing to do with the fact that the aircraft was coming in to land. She was wondering what Liam Brant's reaction would be when he found that Bianca had left the country without a word to him. He was the last man who would take kindly to being made a fool of, and the realisation that Bianca had merely been playing him along with no intention of co-operating over the biography at all could make him very angry indeed.

And that was something Bianca could very well regret, she thought unhappily as the plane's wheels descended smoothly on to the tarmac, and she was aware of a chill that even the brilliant Italian sunshine could not dispel.

CHAPTER FOUR

THERE was a chauffeur-driven limousine to meet them at the airport, and another press contingent to deal with as well. It was over an hour before they were able to get away. It felt stiflingly hot in the airport, but they would be driving up into the hills where it would, with luck, be cooler.

The luggage would be coming in another car, and Monty elected to travel in this, so Alix found herself sitting beside Bianca in the back of the limousine, while Leon took the seat beside the chauffeur.

Alix wondered if she ought to raise the subject of the book with Bianca, but she seemed to be in a pettish mood as she often was after travelling, complaining of the beginnings of a headache, so Alix remained silent.

It was a longer drive than she had expected. She had expected a big house on the fringe of the city, but Rome was behind them now, and the car was climbing steadily into the hills. A shimmer of heat hung over the landscape, and the tall cypresses at the side of the road looked parched and dusty.

Alix was amazed to discover how soon they had left the urban sophistication of the airport and its environs behind them. She stared down into the valley, now opening out beneath them. She could pick out at least two homesteads surrounded by patches of cultivation, but apart from that the land looked arid, covered in rock and scrub.

They drove through a village, its small houses with their peeling wash façades dominated by an enormous pale pink church with cupolas and an elaborate belfry. Some children playing in the dust at the side of the road waved to the car as they went past, and Alix waved back. It was a pity it couldn't have been Bianca, clasping the huge bouquet of flowers which had been awaiting her at the airport, but she was asleep, her mouth set peevishly, and Alix did not dare to wake her.

She would certainly not be pleased to find that Carlo Veronese's villa was so far from the city. The rural life had never appealed to Bianca, and these bare and parched surroundings would be an affront.

On they went, past an isolated farm where excited dogs ran out, sounding an instant alarm, and then after a few miles the car began to descend, somewhat to Alix's relief. She hadn't been looking forward to Bianca's reaction to the news that she was to spend the next few weeks on top of a mountain, which was how it had seemed at first.

She could see that here the valley had been cultivated in terraces, and wondered if there were vines. A group of hikers were tramping steadily across one ploughed patch in a way that would surely have aroused the farmer's wrath in England. Perhaps attitudes were different in Italy, Alix thought, pitying their red perspiring faces and shoulders bowed beneath their backpacks.

They came to another village. The church was smaller this time but equally a monument to the baroque. There was a market in progress in the square, the stalls piled high with huge melons, peaches, tomatoes and peppers. There were a lot of people in the square, wandering between the stalls, standing in chattering groups, fingering the fruit and vegetables, tossing over the bolts of fabric. The chauffeur had to slow right down and proceed with the utmost caution.

Alix leaned forward, tired of her air-conditioned cage, wishing that she could be out in the sunshine, among the sounds and scents of the market.

Perhaps if the villa wasn't too far away—and surely it couldn't be—she could manage to squeeze in a visit while she was here. She would like to explore the church too, she thought appreciatively, turning slightly in her seat and looking back at it, her glance casual at first—then with heart-lurching suddenness hardening into a stare of disbelief as she registered the tall man who had just emerged from its dark interior and was standing at the head of the steps saying something to his companion.

She was seeing things—she was obsessed—she was going insane. There could be no other explanation. Because that could not be Liam Brant standing outside that church talking to the dark-robed priest. It was impossible. It had to be a trick of the light, or a figment of her imagination. She was superimposing his face on to some complete stranger by some psychological quirk she didn't even want to guess at.

She twisted back in her seat, and sat staring ahead of her rigidly, unseeingly, aware that her heart was thumping, and the palms of her hands were damp.

It can't be him, she thought. It can't be. He's in London. He has no idea where we are, so he can't be following us. It's ridiculous even to give it a moment's credence.

It's still the tourist season, although it's late. There must be dozens of tall dark men in the vicinity. I must not let my imagination run away with me.

The car was still going slowly, in fact it had almost slowed to a stop to allow a group of children to scamper across in front of it.

Moving slowly and stiffly as if she was not totally in control of her actions, Alix turned once more to look back at the church. He was still there, but this time his back was turned. Tall, she registered, with dark hair almost to the collar of his white shirt. Slim hips, long legs in tight-fitting denim, a camera over one shoulder. It could be anyone.

And whoever he was, he was not alone. A girl had emerged from the church and was standing looking up at him. Alix saw long blonde hair, and the gleam of a silky texture to the matching deep violet shirt and pants.

There was an impression of confident, vibrant beauty as she tucked a proprietorial hand through his arm.

And then they turned out of the square, and Alix lost sight of them.

She made herself relax, sinking back into the upholstered luxury of the seat. Her second look had been too inconclusive to be totally reassuring, and she could only appeal to her own common sense.

Even if Liam had discovered Bianca's intention to leave, he would hardly have been able to follow so soon. Not that he'd even done that. If the man on the church steps really had been him, it would have meant that he would have preceded them here. And if that was the case—if he really was in pursuit of Bianca—then he would hardly be engaged in casual sightseeing with some gorgeous woman friend in tow.

No—she'd noticed a chance resemblance, and allowed her imagination to gallop away with her.

Bianca was stirring irritably beside her. 'Good God, aren't we there yet? Where in hell are we?'

'We've just come through a village. I'm sure it can't be much farther,' Alix said placatingly. For a moment she considered telling Bianca about her misplaced suspicions, then decided against it. In her present mood, it would be a mistake to tell her anything she might not want to hear.

Bianca seemed all set to work herself into a miniature tantrum.

'What a journey! I shall have something to say to Leon about all this. We should have stayed in Rome, and Carlo Veronese could have come to see me there. He must be mad—burying himself in a remote spot like this.'

'Oh, I don't know,' Alix murmured. 'It's rather wild and beautiful. If you close your eyes, you can imagine meeting a Roman legion coming over the hill.'

Bianca gave a strident laugh. 'Roman legion—the Red Brigade, more likely. Or the Mafia. Anyone could be waiting round the next bend.'

But as it turned out, it was the villa which was waiting there, and the car was already slowing for high wrought iron gates between tall stone pillars, crowned by crouching if rather weatherbeaten lions.

As the car approached, the chauffeur sounded the horn and the gates swung slowly open. Alix, fascinated, supposed they must be controlled electronically, probably from a small building like a lodge just inside the gates.

As they approached the lodge, the car slowed to a crawl. As Alix leaned forward, she saw a face appear at the window, surmounted by a peaked cap, and presumed it must be some kind of security guard, checking on the new arrivals. She supposed she should be used to it by now. So many famous people now surrounded themselves with the trappings of security formerly enjoyed by heads of state or royalty, and for utterly practical reasons, but the very fact that such precautions might be necessary always made Alix shiver. As she sat back in her seat again, the car began to move forward and somewhere close at hand she heard a dog bark menacingly.

The drive ran between banks of flowering shrubs and bushes, interspersed with the darker green of cypresses. Alix, craning her neck to catch a glimpse of some half-concealed piece of statuary, could not help contrasting the apparent luxuriance of the growth in the villa gardens to the poverty of the farmsteads they had passed.

She tried to remember what she had heard about Carlo Veronese and his beginnings in the film industry. One story said he was a street urchin from the slums of Milan. Another said that his father had owned a vineyard. But no one seemed to know what the truth was, and Veronese himself would give no hint.

'If you wish to know me, then watch my films,' he had once barked at an inquisitive journalist. 'That is where I can be found, not in the fantasies of gossip columns.'

Nevertheless, he had featured pretty heavily in a number of such columns over the years with his full-blooded enjoyment of the jet-set life, the parties and the beautiful women. It was almost incredible that he and Bianca should never have met, and Alix could only suppose it was because Veronese did most of his work in Europe, whereas Bianca preferred to spend most of her working life in the United States.

After the grandiose effect of the garden, Alix wasn't sure what to expect from the house itself. In fact the low, rather rambling cream building had an unexpectedly restrained opulence about it. It might be a show place, but it was also very much a home, she thought appraisingly.

Veronese himself was waiting in the paved courtyard in front of the main door to greet them. He was a powerfully built man of something less than medium height, his thick grey-streaked hair just beginning to recede from his temples. It was a strong face, sensual and strongly marked, and his eyes were very dark and bright beneath bushy eyebrows.

Alix thought he looked more like a successful farmer than a film director. Perhaps some of the 'son of the earth' stories weren't so far off target.

He came forward smiling and shook hands with Leon, who introduced him to Bianca. With great deference he took her hand and lifted it to his lips.

'It is an honour, Miss Layton.' His voice was deep and heavily accented. 'A great honour—and also a pleasure.'

His eyes went over the woman in front of him with frank appreciation, and Alix thought, 'Oh, very nicely done,' as she saw the tension begin to drain out of Bianca and saw her smile in response.

'And your companion?' Veronese turned towards Alix.

'My young cousin, Alix Coulter. She acts as my secretary.' Bianca's tone was almost dismissive, and
Veronese's smile widened.

'A cousin? How pleasing for you both. There is
nothing so good as the loyalty and affection of the
family, is it not so? I too have a cousin staying with me,
among other guests. You will be company for each
other.' He turned back towards Bianca. 'I hope you had
a good flight.'

'Dreary as always.' Bianca's tone was rather acid.
'And a much longer car ride than I expected.'

'And it has tired you. You will wish to rest.'
Veronese took her arm. 'My housekeeper Maria Battista
will show you to your suite, and bring you a *tisana*. I
promise that it will banish the tiredness and the aching
from sitting so long. While you are in my house, Miss
Layton, you shall be cherished.'

Alix smothered a grin as she followed in their wake
into the house. 'Bravo, Signor Veronese,' she applauded
silently. 'First round to you!'

The hall seemed to be constructed entirely of marble
in soft blues and greens and cream. It gave an illusion
of coolness, and Alix thought pleasurably how nice it
would be to discard shoes and tights and walk barefoot
across the huge square tiles.

Bianca came to a halt. She began sharply, 'But my
luggage isn't here yet. And nor is Monty. I can't possibly
manage without Monty.'

Veronese was leading her towards the wide, gracious
sweep of the stairs.

'But yes, *cara*, all will be well. Maria Battista will
take care of you. She takes care of everything—you will
see.'

He swung towards a very large woman who had just
materialised beside them, and began to speak to her very
quickly and loudly in Italian. Bianca winced, and put a
hand to her head.

'*La poverina.*' Maria Battista's voice was as soft as

the cooing of doves, and as soothing. In some curious way she seemed to enfold Bianca without even touching her. 'Come with me, *signora*. All is prepared for you.'

And Bianca without another protest went with her, up the stairs and out of sight. Alix watched them go with a sense of disbelief. Monty's real rival could be here, she thought wryly, then realised with a start that Veronese was talking to her.

'And you, *signorina*? Are you also tired, and wish to lie down in your room with the shutters closed, or would you prefer to change and swim in the pool, with perhaps some iced tea to follow?'

Alix smiled. 'That sounds a wonderful idea, but I am a working girl, *signore*, and my—Miss Layton may need me.'

'She will not.' He shook his head very positively. 'Maria Battista will see to it that she sleeps until it is time for her to dress for dinner, and by that time both her luggage and the good dragon who guards her will be here.'

Alix eyed him levelly. 'You seem to know a great deal about Miss Layton and her domestic arrangements.'

His eyes twinkled. 'I think it is a wise general, *signorina*, who surveys the field before the battle.'

Alix raised her eyebrows. 'You're expecting a fight?'

'I never expect such unpleasant things, little one. What I expect is a victory. Now I will go and talk to my good friend, Leon, and later we will meet beside the pool.'

'Just one small snag,' said Alix as he turned to leave. 'I'm also waiting for the luggage.'

He shrugged. 'It is not necessary. Graziella will show you your room, then she will take you down to the pool. In the changing rooms you will find robes, towels and swimming costumes of all shapes and sizes.' He paused, his eyes good-humoured, swiftly all-encompassing. 'I am sure there will be a green one.' He nodded at her and went out into the sunshine.

Graziella was small and shy and she did not speak very much English, but she seemed to understand that Alix was delighted with her room, and share in her pleasure.

The floor tiles were predominantly white, with flecks of gold and turquoise, and the hangings in the room, at the windows and on the bed were pale turquoise too. The walls were white and so was the furniture. The windows opened on to a tiny balcony, weighted down with bougainvillea, and overlooking another section of the garden, this time set out in formal style with flower beds, and walks and small clipped hedges, and in the centre a sundial. It had a formal air, the air of another time, another age, as if it had lain dreaming under several centuries of hot Italian sunlight. And yet that was hardly possible, Alix thought, because surely the villa was comparatively modern. As she watched, Carlo Veronese and Leon came into view, obviously deep in conversation. Leon's head was bent, and his hands were clasped behind his back as he paced along beside his companion, who was gesticulating excitedly in order to emphasise some point he was making.

Alix was going to call to them, but they were too far away to hear her, she decided on second thoughts, and probably much too absorbed in whatever they were discussing. It had to be business because they both looked so serious, she thought, but then if they were discussing the Francesca film, it was a serious subject. It was going to be a high-budget major production, and no detail about it could be glossed over lightly.

She turned back into the room to find Graziella waiting to show her down to the swimming pool, a fact she conveyed with a few words of broken English and some vivid sign language.

Alix supposed she should really report to Bianca, and see if there was anything she wanted, but she soothed her conscience with the reflection that Bianca was obviously in safe hands with Maria Battista and would not welcome an interruption if she was resting. Besides, Monty would be arriving soon, and Bianca would be wanting to bathe and change for dinner, rather than requiring the services of her secretary.

The pool was at the back of the house behind a tall cypress hedge, and reached by the steps of a paved terrace.

The changing rooms were housed in a low white building with a green tiled roof at one end of the pool. The area round the pool was paved in turquoise and white, and padded sun-loungers in shades of coral and turquoise with matching sun-umbrellas were set at intervals around it.

Alix was rather glad to see that none of them were currently occupied, and that she would have the pool to herself for a little while at least.

Graziella took her into the changing cabin and showed her where everything was kept. As Veronese had indicated, there were plenty of swimsuits to choose from, and Alix had already reached for a plain black one-piece when Graziella took her arm, shaking her head vigorously. It was clear she wanted Alix to choose the bikini she was holding out to her with a persuasive smile. As far as Alix could see it consisted of a few brief triangles of jade green and gold, fastened with slender jade green cords, and it was far skimpier than anything she had ever worn.

At first she refused smilingly, but Graziella's disappointment was so obvious that she allowed herself to relent, and replaced the black costume on its hanger in the long cupboard. After all, there was no one to see her, she told herself.

Nevertheless, she could not help a twinge of selfconsciousness when she emerged from the cubicle, and caught a glimpse of herself in the full-length mirror on one of the walls.

The bikini made only the briefest concessions to decency, she thought wryly, but she could not deny that it became her. Even Graziella had vanished, so she was completely alone as she emerged from the changing room with a towel draped over her arm.

Graziella had shown her where all the sun preparations were kept too, but those she had left where they were. She would enjoy a quick swim. The sparkling turquoise water looked infinitely inviting, but she wouldn't be sunbathing afterwards until she had found something less revealing to wear.

She slid into the water, revelling in its chill on her heated skin. She swam well with an easy overarm stroke, and she managed a length without effort before turning on her back and floating for a while, staring up at the perfect blue arc of the sky through half-closed eyes.

At Bianca's house in California, she swam in the pool every day, although Bianca rarely used it, claiming that the water ruined her hair, and that too much exercise would over-develop her muscles.

Alix completed a couple of widths of the pool in a leisurely back-stroke, then turned a supple somersault and began to swim under the water. A few minutes only, she promised herself, then she would shower and dress and go back to the villa. It was a long time since she had enjoyed herself so much in the water. There had been a pool at the hotel in Rhodes, but it had always been crowded, even in the evenings. The most she had managed was the occasional dip to cool down after sunbathing. To be alone like this was a rare luxury.

She surfaced at the side of the pool, the sun glinting against her closed eyelids, her hands reaching up for the ladder to pull herself up and out. But instead of the expected smooth metal rail, her fingers closed on warm flesh and bone. Strong hands which slid along her arms, and down to her waist, to lift her bodily out of the water and deposit her on the cool tiles. Hands which sent a long shiver of awareness down her body.

She was gasping with shock, recoiling furiously as she tried to shake the water out of her eyes, and her wet feet slipped on the tiles and she might have fallen, except those unknown hands were there again, under her elbows, supporting her until she regained her balance.

She opened her eyes and stared up unbelievingly into the face of the man who held her.

She whispered, 'You? But it can't be!'

Liam said, 'Oh, but it is, secretary bird. My compliments, by the way, on the new plumage.'

Alix stood staring at him. She felt a curious sense of unreality as if she were running a fever. She had known as soon as she felt his touch who it must be, and yet it still didn't seem possible. Nor did the surge of excitement, of pleasure which was welling up within her. Those were dangerous emotions, and she had to be on her guard against them—against him.

And just then she realised what he had said, and felt herself blushing hotly as she remembered how little she was wearing.

She said hurriedly, 'How did you get in here?' as she looked round wildly to see where she had left her towel.

His brows rose and he looked faintly amused. 'In the same way as you did, I would imagine.'

She saw the towel, lying across a lounger, and dived for it, wrapping it around herself defensively.

She said between her teeth, 'I doubt that. I'd advise you to get out of here before Bianca finds out.'

He was smiling openly now. 'You mean she wouldn't be pleased to see me? How very unfortunate!'

Alix said warmly, 'She isn't the only one who won't be pleased. This is a private house, and Carlo Veronese clearly values his privacy. You'd better leave before he has you thrown out.'

'You have a very violent imagination, secretary bird.'

'It has nothing to do with imagination. He has strict security precautions and he won't be pleased to find they've been flouted.'

Liam's mouth twisted slightly. 'Thanks for the warnings, but they're not necessary. You seem to be under a misapprehension. Didn't Carlo mention that he had other guests?'

She felt her jaw drop. Struggling for her composure, she said, 'You mean—you're staying here too? But you can't be!'

'Can't I?' he said pleasantly. 'Not everyone finds me as unacceptable as you do, Miss Coulter. Although for a moment back there, I actually thought you might be softening a little.'

She felt her breathing quicken. What had she let him see? she wondered. 'Well, think again, Mr Brant,' she returned with all the calmness she could muster. 'Do you really expect me to believe that you just happen to have been invited here at this particular time?'

'No,' he said. 'That would be stretching coincidence too far. But Carlo is an old friend, and he owes me one, so when I suggested it would be useful for the book if I sat in on the preliminary discussions for this film, he was happy to agree.'

'And do you imagine for one moment that Bianca will be—happy to agree?'

'On the contrary,' he said, 'if the way she studiously avoided all mention of the trip is anything to go by. But as I think I already hinted to you, while I'd prefer her co-operation, it isn't essential.'

'Well, I think you're being most unfair,' she said hotly. 'This film is an important one, and Bianca doesn't need your kind of hassle.'

'I think we can leave fairness out of the discussion. If it comes to it, she hasn't been altogether fair to me. She tried to pull the wool over my eyes in London, only it didn't work. I was ahead of her all the way.' His voice was cold suddenly, and in spite of the sun's heat, she shivered, wrapping the towel which had slipped slightly more closely round her slender body.

Liam noticed the gesture, and smiled mockingly. 'Don't be coy,' he advised lazily. 'If you don't want to be looked at, you shouldn't put the goods in the window.'

'I wasn't aware I had done so.'

'No? Then obviously you also don't know how provocative your current cover-up tactics are.'

Before she could stir or make a move to prevent him he reached out and pulled the towel away from her, tossing it behind him.

'How dare you!' Alix choked.

'Oh, don't be such a fool,' he said impatiently. 'You don't need the towel. You can't be cold in this heat, and if you're damp, the sun will soon dry you. The only other arguments are that you're ashamed of your body, which can't be true, or that you're super-modest, which doesn't fit with your choice of swim-wear.'

'It doesn't happen to be my choice,' she said. 'I borrowed it because my own luggage hadn't arrived.'

'And of course, this was the only one available,' he said silkily. 'I think you've made another Freudian slip, secretary bird. Or did you think your borrowed plumes would turn you into a bird of paradise for a while?'

She wanted to protest, to say that she had assumed she would be alone at the swimming pool, but the words wouldn't come suddenly, and if they had, she doubted whether her dry mouth could have uttered them.

With total awareness, she was watching him watching her, and she knew she was afraid. Knew also that beneath the fear was a growing and unquenchable excitement. Found she couldn't explain either the fear or the excitement, and as he took one long irrevocable step towards her, knew that she didn't even want to.

His hands closed on her waist, but lightly so that she could have pulled free, but she didn't. His hands moved on her gently, silk against velvet, travelling downwards until they rested on the smooth curve of her hips, and when she did move, it was towards him. His gaze touched hers, held it, then dropped slowly to her lips, and down to her breasts, barely concealed by the tiny silken jade triangles, with all the potency of a caress.

A voice inside her head was whispering feverishly, *'Kiss me. Oh God, please kiss me!'*

But as her lips parted, the only sound she uttered was a long quivering sigh, and her lashes fluttered down on to her cheeks, helplessly, submissively as the dark head bent towards her.

At first, his mouth brushed hers gently as a butterfly's wing, as tantalising as a summer breeze, and it was not enough—she wanted more as she swayed forward until the tips of her breasts touched the hard muscular wall of his body in an almost intolerable friction.

Liam must have been aware of her arousal, yet he made no apparent attempt to deepen his caresses, at least not at first. Instead, he laid a trail of little kisses on her eyelids, her temples, the corners of her mouth, and the soft throbbing pulse in her throat before returning once more to her mouth, his tongue stroking gently and sensually along the swollen fullness of her lower lip.

His hand lifted slowly to cradle the nape of her neck, his fingers opening a path of bewitchment from the lobe of her ear, down the curve of her throat to her shoulder.

Alix was trembling, her breathing suddenly shallow and erratic as she fought to retain some semblance of sanity. She had been kissed before, but never with this slow, insidious beguilement which was transforming her shaking body into one long ache of yearning. She was confused too. She wanted the evidence that the passion he was rousing in her was reciprocated. She wanted his arms to hold her tightly, the pressure of his mouth to deepen, she wanted to venture into realms which as yet existed only in her imagination, she wanted to unlock for him all the treasures of the innocent kingdom she had hitherto guarded with such care—guarded, she realised now, just for this moment, and this man.

She arched herself blindly towards him, lifting her arms up round his neck. She heard the huskiness of her own voice as she whispered, 'Love me.'

And felt unbelievably him step away from her. Her

clinging arms were detached, and she was set at a distance—a small one, it was true, but no less chilling for that.

Her eyes flew open in shock and met his. He was smiling rather oddly, and his voice was cool as he said, 'An enlightening interlude—for both of us, I'd say. What a pity it has to end so soon.'

Alix thought she would die of shame. The tenderness she had imagined in his kiss, in his touch had vanished, and only mockery remained. She lifted her hands and pressed them against her burning cheeks, as she registered the implications of what had happened. An interlude, he had said. That was all. He wasn't a fool. He had picked up her physical awareness of him, and decided to indulge it for a while—as if she was a child to be placated with sweets, because she wasn't old enough for more adult enjoyments.

She said, 'On the contrary, it was a pity it ever began.'

His mouth twisted. 'That's an attitude that belongs with a crinoline, darling, and not with the few square inches of material that you're wearing. Haven't you realised that our rather dubious privacy is about to be invaded?'

She hadn't realised anything of the sort, she thought miserably, because she'd been aware of nothing but him. She could hear the voices and the approaching footsteps now, of course. She only wished she had heard them minutes before, and that she had been the one to step back, before she allowed herself to utter that disastrous and humiliating plea.

She went past him and picked up her towel, trying to conceal the fact that she was still shaking.

Carlo said genially, 'So here you are, my friends. Tell me, Miss Coulter—no, I cannot call you that—so cold, so formal. I shall call you Alix, is it not so? Did you enjoy your swim?'

'It was wonderful,' Alix managed to inject a note of

false enthusiasm into her voice. 'Just what I needed.'
She didn't even glance at Liam. Instead her gaze was
riveted on the girl who had accompanied Carlo. Long
blonde hair and violet silk made her instantly recognis-
able. What Alix hadn't fully appreciated from the car
was her beauty. Her skin was the colour of honey, and
her eyes were golden brown fringed by long lashes arti-
ficially darkened. She had a small straight nose, and a
smiling, voluptuously curved mouth.

'This is my little Paola,' Carlo announced. 'I know
that you two will be friends.'

Alix doubted it. Paola's smile was perfectly amiable
as she greeted Alix, and murmured that it was a pleasure
to meet her, but that was as far as it went. Paola was a
man's woman, and every sidelong look from those
amazing eyes, every movement of that perfectly curved
body proclaimed the fact, to her own evident satisfaction.

She replied to Paola's civil questions on whether this
was her first visit to Italy with equal politeness and
popped in a question of her own.

'Did you enjoy your sightseeing this afternoon?'

For a moment Paola looked blank, and then she
laughed. 'Ah—the village. That church.' She gave a
charming shrug. 'Perhaps—but one church is like another. It is Liam who is interested in such things, not I.'
Smiling, she drifted towards Liam and kissed him on
the cheek. 'Ciao, caro.'

Alix found herself saying stiltedly, 'If you'll excuse
me, I must go and get dressed. Bianca will be wondering
where I am.'

'I don't think so. Miss Montgomery has arrived and
is with her. I have asked Giovanni to bring drinks down
to the pool. We are going to swim now. Stay with us,'
Carlo urged.

'No, really.' Alix shook her head. 'If—if Monty is
here, that means the luggage is here too, and I should
unpack—retrieve my own swimwear,' she added rather
wildly.

Carlo's smile widened. 'Why, when the one you have chosen is so suitable and so becoming? But if you insist, then we must let you go. Maria Battista will bring your iced tea to your room. Ring when you are ready for it.'

Alix thanked him, and hurriedly fetched her clothes from the changing room, wrapping the towel round her like a sarong while she made her way indoors.

When she reached her room, she found that her case had already been unpacked, and her belongings stowed in the row of fitted wardrobes which filled one wall, while her toiletries had been bestowed in the pink and ivory bathroom which opened off the bedroom. Early in her career as Bianca's secretary, she had learned that it was part of her duties to travel lightly, and that it was her aunt who was always surrounded by a complete set of matched luggage.

Consequently, the few clothes she had brought with her looked rather lost in all that space.

And that's just as it should be, Alix thought forlornly, as she stripped off the bikini with something like loathing, and wrapped herself in her cotton housecoat. Because she herself felt lost and utterly alone.

CHAPTER FIVE

A cool shower and the promised iced tea revived her a little. She chose a dress to wear to dinner, then put it back and picked another one at random, tossing it on to the bed. It wasn't as in any way becoming as her first choice, but that was all to the good. She was here to work, which was something she had lost sight of for a while.

She had come disastrously close to making a complete fool of herself in Liam's arms. He had been right when he said it had been enlightening. It had enlightened Alix as to how dangerously lacking in sophistication she was. His jibe about the crinoline had been well founded, she thought, flushing. Her every reaction had been Victorian, and it was no excuse to blame the devastating and unexpected effect he had had on her senses and emotions. She had behaved like a naïve schoolgirl, when all Liam had wanted was a few moments' amusement before his girlfriend showed up.

It was little wonder he couldn't wait to get her out of his arms, and no wonder at all that his antennae had been so finely tuned to the others' approach. He had been expecting them.

How embarrassed he must have been when she threw herself at him, Alix thought, deliberately mortifying himself. The last thing he wanted was her clinging to him when Paola was only a few yards away. She was probably like a tigress when her jealousy and anger were aroused.

She had shampooed her hair while she was in the shower, and now she sat on the dressing stool near the open window, blowing the soft strands dry with a hairdryer she had discovered in one of the bathroom cupboards. She found the action soothing, but at the same time she could not help despising herself. New washed hair, however soft and shining, was no competition for Paola's dazzling blonde beauty.

But she wasn't competing, anyway, she reminded herself forcefully. From the moment she had met Liam, she had been attracted and disturbed by him, but she had to face the fact that the attraction was all on her side. He had kissed her probably because she had signalled so unmistakably that she wanted to be kissed, she acknowledged wryly, and because she had been next door to naked. But it had been the impulse of a moment with him, and certainly not a sign that he wanted any deeper kind of relationship with her.

She switched off the hairdryer and laid it down, wondering as she do so how Liam had kissed Bianca. Had his mouth moved over her face in the same gentle sensuous exploration, or with a surging passion which would have demanded and obtained an equal response?

She shivered, catching the softness of her lower lip fiercely between her teeth. There was no place in her life for such speculation, when it brought this kind of pain in its wake. It was none of her business what Liam did with Bianca. He was a man of the world, and presumably took his pleasure where he found it without commitment. In this, he and Bianca were two of a kind. All the same, Alix couldn't guarantee that her mercurial aunt would accept with equanimity his reappearance in her life with a much younger and equally glamorous girlfriend in tow.

A line from an old Hollywood film she had seen on television and enjoyed came forcibly into her mind. *'Fasten your seat-belts. It's going to be a bumpy ride.'*

She brushed her hair so that it swung in a shining curve around her face, and applied her usual minimal makeup with maximum care and attention, highlighting her eyes and cheekbones.

Her dress was russet brown in a soft crêpe material

with a full skirt and long sleeves edged by deep cuffs in
cream broderie anglaise, with a matching collar at the
high neck. It dated from her demure period, but was
none the worse for that, Alix thought with a little sigh.
Demureness was easier to handle than provocation
any day. Besides, she didn't want to add to what was
threatening to turn into an explosive situation by aggra-
vating Bianca.

And that's not cowardice, she told herself with a kind
of desperate gaiety, it's self-preservation.

Giovanni was waiting in the hall when she went down
the stairs and he showed her into a large *salotto* where
cocktails were waiting, he told her.

It was a beautiful room, Alix thought approvingly.
One wall seemed composed entirely of glass, with
windows which opened on to the terrace. Its focal point
was a raised fireplace in the centre of the room, unlit at
this time of year, with a dramatic copper canopy above
it. Further drama was supplied by the pictures which
hung on the plain cream walls. Most of them were
modern and abstract, but among them Alix thought she
recognised a Cézanne.

Apart from Giovanni, expertly mixing her the dry
Martini she had asked for, the only other occupant of
the room was Leon, sitting on one of the low silk-
covered sofas and gazing into a gin and tonic as if it
was a crystal ball with bad news.

She felt sorry for him. Leon was a business man first
and last. He had handled Bianca's career and contracts
with flair, but he had little idea how to cope with her on
a personal level, Alix had often suspected. He was a
happily married man who enjoyed sailing and golf
with his family at weekends, and Alix had often
thought that Bianca's way of living her life shocked
him, and outraged his conventional sense of morality.
He would be totally baffled by the undercurrents at
the villa.

As she took her drink with a murmured word of

thanks and moved over to sit opposite him, Leon gave her a frankly worried look.

'This is a pretty kettle of fish,' he muttered.

Alix found herself wondering which particular section of the whole mess he was referring to. It was like Leon to use an outdated metaphor like that, she thought. It was the kind of thing which so often in the past had led business rivals and opponents to underestimate him—to their cost.

Now he said ruefully, 'I've slipped up this time, Alix. By the time we leave here, Bianca will be looking for a new agent.'

'Of course she won't,' said Alix, soothing but startled. 'You couldn't possibly have known.'

He passed a hand wearily over his thinning hair. 'Thanks for the testimonial, my dear, but it just isn't true. I should have known. It's what I'm paid for.'

To keep track of Bianca's former lovers, and their new relationships? He couldn't be serious, Alix thought bewilderedly. But Leon wasn't joking, and rarely did anyway. He was a worried man, and showing it, which was a very different reaction from his usual twitch of distaste over Bianca's emotional involvements and their inevitable aftermath.

Of course, her involvement with Liam hadn't been totally emotional. There was also the book which Bianca imagined she had successfully managed to shelve. She might well feel that Leon who had set up this meeting with Veronese should have checked to find out who else was going to be there.

And yet what could Leon have done? Alix thought. It was Veronese's house. He was entitled to invite anyone he liked, even if he was pressured into it. And Bianca really wanted this film. A cartload of vindictive ex-husbands wouldn't have kept her away, let alone one unwanted biographer.

She said tentatively, 'I'm sure you're exaggerating. It's—unfortunate, I admit, but . . .'

'Unfortunate?' he echoed, his pale eyes staring at her as if she had suddenly grown an extra head. 'My God, Alix, you don't realise . . .' He stopped abruptly, closing his mouth tightly as the door at the far end of the room opened and Carlo Veronese entered smiling.

'Giovanni has been looking after you both? Good, good. I am sorry I was not here, but I was called to the telephone. You know how it is. Leon, you have finished your drink. Let me fix you another. Alix, *cara*, how charming you look tonight.'

Alix watched astonished as Leon accepted another gin and tonic. He must be upset, she thought, because he could usually make one drink last an entire session. He was famous for setting up liquid lunches for other people, and adroit at avoiding the consequences himself. She hoped she wasn't going to have to cope with a drunken Leon as well as everything else.

In an attempt to draw attention from his glum expression, she asked Carlo about the pictures and he was delighted, drawing her hand through his arm and leading her round the room as he talked about them. He was knowledgeable, but what warmed Alix was the evident fact that he was not merely a collector for art's sake, but genuinely loved the paintings he had chosen. She wasn't sure she shared his taste completely, but she couldn't fail to be interested in what he had to say.

Although she didn't hear the door open, she knew exactly when Liam entered the room by the prickle of awareness which lifted the hair on the back of her neck. Hidden in the folds of her skirt, her hands balled into fists and she felt consumed by tension as she smiled and nodded and listened without hearing to what Carlo was saying about the Post-Impressionists.

'Giving one of your art lessons, Carlo?' His voice just behind them sounded amused.

Carlo laughed goodhumouredly. 'And why not, my friend? It isn't often I have so charming, and so captive an audience.'

Alix went on staring at the painting so fixedly, she thought she could probably reproduce every brushmark from memory. He was standing so close to her that she could feel the warmth from his body, and her legs were weak as if her bones were dissolving.

And he knew, she thought hating both him and herself. He would know from her response by the pool, exactly what effect he was having on her. Well, she was damned if she would let him see that he could manipulate her like some helpless marionette!

She turned slowly, her eyes steady, her smile cool, and those betraying clenched hands well hidden.

'Are you interested in art, Mr Brant?' The use of the surname moved him to a distance for her, mentally if not physically.

His expression was sardonic as if he could read her mind.

'Yes—without considering myself a connoisseur of any particular period or style. In Italy of course that isn't necessary. There are riches on all sides from every age.'

'But this Alix will know already,' Carlo put it. 'You have been to Italy before, *cara*? You have seen Florence—Venice—Rome?'

She shook her head. 'I'm afraid not. This is my first visit, and it isn't a sightseeing trip.' She could have added that as far as Bianca was concerned the entire glory of Bernini, Michelangelo, Titian, Canaletto and everyone else could be laid out for her inspection and she would pass by without a second glance. Lester Marchant had tried unavailingly to get her to take an interest in painting, and to invest in it. Bianca herself preferred jewellery, which Alix privately considered rather soulless.

'But you will not be working all the time. Even the most conscientious secretary deserves some hours to herself. We will have to see what can be arranged. We cannot let her visit Italy for the first time and see nothing of the treasures of the past, can we, Liam?'

Alix felt her polite smile freeze on her lips. 'Not this time, I'm afraid. Bianca really does keep me busy, you see.'

'At her London home, when you are in America, yes.' Carlo was clearly puzzled. 'But here, there cannot be so much for you to do.'

Except be at her beck and call all day long, whenever the mood takes her, Alix thought but did not say.

'Even when she's travelling, she likes to deal with her correspondence,' she prevaricated smoothly. 'I'll make a special trip some time.'

'A package tour,' Liam said softly. 'All the art centres of Europe in ten days with a coachload of other culture vultures.'

She glared at him silently, knowing that he was simply trying to provoke her. Ever since childhood, she had dreamed of seeing Italy—Venice particularly. However commercialised, however crumbling, however odorous in high summer, La Serenissima had an aura of romance about it which had always silently called to her. She could have afforded a holiday there easily since she had started working for Bianca. She had even considered it on a couple of occasions, and yet something had always stopped her. Something which told her that Venice was not a city to be visited in solitude. It was impossible to imagine oneself in a gondola alone, or feeding the pigeons in the Piazza San Marco without having someone there to share the fun of it. But she had never had any clear idea of the person she wanted to take her to Venice.

At least not until now, she thought painfully.

'Oh, we will have to plan something more exciting than that,' Carlo was saying. 'She is a dear girl, our little Alix. She likes my pictures, or at least she does not say that she dislikes them.' And he chuckled.

'She's certainly very discreet,' Liam said drily. His eyes went over her, leaving her in little doubt about what he thought of her dress. 'Or she is most of the time.'

'Now you're being enigmatic, my friend,' Carlo accused jovially. 'We will not ask what you mean, I think. Instead I will get you a drink. Your usual whisky and water?'

'Thanks,' Liam nodded, still watching Alix. She felt the colour beginning to rise in her face and made to turn away, but he reached out a hand and took her arm, stopping her in her tracks.

'Where are you running to now?' he asked.

'I wasn't aware I was running anywhere,' she said stiffly. 'I was going to talk to Leon. I think he's in need of some company.' And also apparently in need of yet another gin and tonic, she noticed with alarm.

His face was sardonic. 'And I don't need company, of course.'

'I'd have thought this villa contains more than you can handle already,' she muttered.

'Presumably you know what you mean by that. I don't, but nor do I intend to enquire.' He put out a finger and flicked at the broderie anglaise collar. 'I see the Puritan age has returned. You really do go from one extreme to the other, don't you, secretary bird?'

'If you say so.' She gave a slight shrug. 'I forgot— you're an expert on women's clothes. I suppose you know exactly how I should be dressed.'

'What interests me far more,' he said, 'is knowing exactly how you should be undressed. In fact, I can hardly wait.'

Alix gasped and stepped back slightly, spilling a little of her drink down her skirt as she did so.

'Oh, look what you've made me do!' she exclaimed distressfully.

'Don't expect me to apologise,' he said. 'If it means that you're going to change out of that rag into something that befits the woman we both know you're capable of being, then that's all to the good.'

'I haven't the slightest intention of changing,' she said coldly. 'This material fortunately doesn't stain.'

'I could make a whole list of the things it doesn't do,' he said pleasantly. 'Would you like to hear some of them?'

'No!' she almost spat at him. 'Oh, why can't you leave me alone?'

'Because I don't want to, and if you're honest you'll admit that isn't what you want either.' His voice was cool. 'I have an excellent memory—almost total recall, in fact—but even if I hadn't, I'd hardly have forgotten what you said to me at the pool this afternoon, just before we were interrupted. Or do you need to be reminded?'

'No.' She glanced around desperately for Carlo, willing him to return with Liam's drink, but he was deep in conversation with Leon.

'Good,' he approved mockingly. 'I'm relieved to know you don't issue such invitations indiscriminately.'

'It wasn't intended as an invitation.' Her voice was almost inaudible. 'I—I didn't know what I was saying . . .' Her voice stopped abruptly as she realised too late what a damaging admission that was.

'But you know what you're saying now,' his voice was dangerously soft. 'And I challenge you, Alix, to look me in the face and tell me you didn't mean it. That the invitation is withdrawn. That you don't want me.'

It could hardly have been simpler, she thought. He'd even told her the words to use, so why didn't she speak? Almost compulsively, she moistened her dry lips with the tip of her tongue as she fought for utterance.

His voice became softer still. 'I said—look at me, Alix.'

She couldn't. That was the impossible condition. There was no way she could lift her eyes to his and risk him reading the misery and uncertainty and frank yearning that he might see there.

And as she hesitated, salvation came with the opening of the door and Bianca's voice. 'Darlings, am I late? Have I kept you all waiting?'

They all swung towards her as if she had been a magnet. She was dazzling tonight in an emerald green silk dress, the slender skirt deeply slashed from the hem to above the knee, and wide straps rising from the low-cut bodice to cross each other before fastening in a halter around her neck. Her dark hair was almost completely hidden beneath an exotically swathed turban in matching silk, and her hands and arms were bare except for a bracelet of emeralds set in white gold on her left wrist.

She stood in the doorway for a moment, then came forward smiling and extending her hands to Carlo, who kissed each of them in turn. It was a perfect entrance, perfectly executed, Alix thought wryly. Yet she herself couldn't even manage one simple line.

Not that it mattered now. Liam had gone to join Leon and Carlo, like satellites around some radiant planet.

Alix watched apprehensively to see what her reaction was, but if Liam's unexpected appearance had thrown her, Bianca gave no sign of it. On the contrary.

'Liam, darling!' Her voice had an intimate throatiness. 'Why didn't you tell me? We could have travelled together.'

He smiled. 'I wanted to surprise you,' he said smoothly. 'And I actually arrived several days ago.'

'So that was why you didn't answer any of my calls.' Bianca sounded reproachful, and the smile she gave him was almost wistful.

Alix had seen it happening many times before. It was what she called Bianca's silken thread in operation. A man might not even realise that it held him, until with one twitch she brought him back to the delights of her captivity.

She couldn't just let them go, Alix had realised a long time ago. She couldn't just let them slide away into oblivion. They had to be kept at the end of the thread until Bianca herself chose to cut it.

Only Liam, it seemed, had come dangerously near to breaking free of his own accord.

Alix lifted her glass and drank what was left in it in one swift gulp. He certainly wouldn't be allowed to escape again. And his captivity promised her freedom.

'Alix, my pet!' Bianca was floating towards her now. 'You look positively wan. Has the journey destroyed you? You shouldn't have come down, darling. Monty's having a tray in her room. I'm sure Carlo would arrange for you to do the same.'

The tone was one of sweet concern, but Bianca's eyes were as hard as agates. What had she seen as she paused in the doorway? Alix wondered. Had she noticed her with Liam, and summed up the situation with her usual shrewdness? It hardly seemed likely. And yet with Bianca one never knew.

Suddenly Alix was angry. She would not be sent to her room like a naughty child, although the girl she had been until a few weeks ago would undoubtedly have submitted to so palpable a hint.

'I'm perfectly fine, thank you,' she returned. 'Signor Veronese is in the middle of telling me about his collection of paintings.'

'Oh, really?' Bianca's smile was a little rigid. 'Carlo darling, you really mustn't let this child impose on you just because she happens to be my cousin. She is also my employee, and is here to work.'

'As she has emphasised to me several times already,' Carlo said calmly. 'If she is a little pale, a good dinner and some red wine will soon return the colour to her cheeks, I think. Besides, I wish her to become better acquainted with Paola, and she cannot do that if she goes to eat in her room.'

Bianca gave a little silvery laugh. 'I don't quite follow. Who is Paola?'

Carlo shrugged. 'A cousin of mine, *cara*. And here she is.'

In its way it was an even better entrance because it appeared to be totally unstudied. Paola wore white, a slip of a dress reaching to her ankles, which fastened on one shoulder in a broad mother-of-pearl strap, leaving the other bare. Alix thought that apart from her shoes, the dress was almost certainly all that Paola was wearing.

She glanced at Bianca to see how she was taking the new arrival and saw something she could not name flicker for a moment in her face before the smiling mask descended again.

She said gaily, 'A cousin, did you say, darling? How enchanting! How fortunate we both are in having such attractive relations.'

'I think so too,' Carlo said blandly. 'And now shall we go in to dinner?'

It was in several ways a memorable meal. The food was delicious—ice-cold melon and Parma ham, followed by veal with mushrooms and herbs cooked in a delicate white wine sauce, but Alix found her appetite had deserted her.

She was seated next to Paola at the big circular table in the dining room. Across the expanse of dark, shining wood she could see Liam, leaning back in his chair, his fingers idly playing with the stem of his wine glass, his face shadowed and enigmatic. Bianca was in the chair next to him, talking and laughing with an almost feverish vivacity, although Alix noticed she wasn't eating much either. She was too busy being the life and soul of a singularly lifeless and soulless party.

There were undercurrents around that table which Alix couldn't even begin to fathom, but she guessed somehow that they were centred in the girl who sat beside her, barely speaking, as golden and serene as a Botticelli goddess.

One explanation could be that Bianca now knew that Paola was involved with Liam, and was jealous, but Alix could not believe it. Bianca never allowed such a mundane emotion to stand in her way. She brooked no interference from other women in her relationships, and her methods were ruthless.

Paola was a beautiful and sexy girl, but there was a basic docility about her, Alix thought, which did not augur well for her in any battles of will with Bianca over Liam or anything else.

She wanted to ask Leon what he thought, but although he was sitting next to her, any private conversation was out of the question. He was still drinking, she realised, and looking more morose with every minute that passed. By the time dinner was finished, she doubted whether he would be capable of telling her anything coherent.

Only Carlo seemed to be behaving normally, eating and drinking with gusto, roaring with laughter at Bianca's anecdotes, and capping them with some of his own, spicing the conversation with scandalous snippets about well-known figures in the film world.

A marvellous performance, Alix thought detachedly. If he hadn't been a famous director, he could have made a good living as an actor. Because she had no doubt it was all an act. He wasn't an insensitive man. He must be attuned to the inner tensions and vibrations around the table, but he was choosing to ignore them, perhaps in the hope that they would go away.

Some hope, Alix reflected bitterly. Almost involuntarily she found she was looking at Liam. It was safe to do so. He was mostly watching Bianca, although his gaze sometimes flickered to Paola.

Judging his options? she surmised painfully. She knew she ought to hate him—despise him for being a womaniser, for not being able to resist the temptation of practising his all too potent sexuality on any female who strayed within his orbit. He doesn't need me, she thought miserably, he probably doesn't even want me as a person. It's the chase and the conquest that matters to him. He challenged me to look him in the face and say I didn't want him. That's all it was to him, a challenge. He wanted me to admit that he'd won.

At least she'd been spared that, but the victory was his all the same, and he knew it.

Even as the thought formed in her mind, Liam turned his head, and across the table their gazes caught and held. Alix felt as if she was turned to stone. She wanted to look away, to look down, to look anywhere except into the watchful dark eyes of the man opposite her. But it was useless. She could not tear herself away, and deep within her that hungry little spiral of excitement was beginning slowly to uncoil until she felt as if every nerve ending in her body was being stretched to screaming point.

She was beginning dazedly to think she would have to scream to break the spell he was winding round her, when Giovanni came in to clear the plates and bring in the dessert.

Alix leaned back in her chair, almost sagging with relief. It had been a prosaic diversion, but effective.

She became aware that Paola was speaking to her.

'Don't you want your food? It's very good.' Her eyes sharpened as she studied Alix. 'Are you feeling well? You look flushed.'

'That has to be an improvement,' Alix muttered. 'Before dinner I looked pale and wan.' She saw Paola's surprised look and made a placatory gesture with her hand. 'I'm sorry, I'm talking nonsense. You're right— the food is delicious. I adore black cherries, especially hot.'

Paola went on watching her, clearly puzzled, as Alix spooned some of the cherries into her mouth, washing them past the tightness in her throat with surreptitious sips of wine.

At last she said, 'Carlo tells me that you are related to Miss Layton as well as her secretary. That you know her well. What is she like?'

On the surface it seemed an artless enough question, but the fact that it was being asked at all made Alix wary, and she stiffened slightly.

Paola laughed. '*Dio*, but Liam was right! He said that she had two dragons to guard her, and that of the two of them you were the most formidable.'

'Oh, did he?' Alix murmured, putting down her spoon. 'Then I'm sure he will also have had something to say about Bianca.'

Paola gave a slight shrug. 'You mean—because he is writing a book about her? But that has hardly begun. He is not pleased with the progress he is making. He thinks she is a mass of contradictions.'

'She's that all right,' Alix made herself speak lightly. 'But if that's all he's managed to find out, it won't make much of a book.'

'Oh, he will find more,' Paola said positively. 'He is a very persistent man—very determined, don't you think?'

'I hardly know him,' said Alix on a little snap which she instantly regretted. She tried to cover it up with a question of her own. 'How did you meet him?'

Paola's eyes slid away. 'We were introduced—by a mutual friend.'

Consider myself snubbed, Alix thought wryly. Aloud she said, 'You speak very good English.'

'*Grazie,*' Paola said demurely, looking amused. 'For most of my life, I have spoken little else. My mother and father lived in the U.S.A. and later in Britain, and I went to school there.'

She mentioned the name of the school, and Alix was duly impressed. She began to suspect that there might be more to Paola than the considerable amount which met the eye, and that the apparent docility could be just good manners instead.

Life with Bianca made one forget that such things existed, Alix thought drily.

'I am glad that you are here, Alix,' Paola was saying, as she finished the last of her cherries. 'I'd expected to be quite bored, but we can swim together—and play tennis.'

Bored—with Liam around? Alix wondered.

Aloud, she said, 'I'm not very good at tennis, I'm afraid.'

Paola laughed. 'Nor am I. But it was better than playing netball—and lacrosse,' she added with a slight grimace.

Alix laughed too. 'In my case, hockey,' she confessed. They smiled at each other, tentatively but genuinely, and Alix was left with the feeling that perhaps the dinner hadn't been a total disaster after all.

They went back to the *salotto* for coffee. The room was full of lamplight, and the long cream curtains had been drawn across the windows to deter the moths and other flying creatures. The curtains stirred faintly in the night breeze, revealing that the terrace door still stood open.

Maria Battista handed round tiny cups full of the rich dark brew and Giovanni served brandy and liqueurs. Paola went over to a large antique chest that stood against one wall and lifted the lid. After a second or two, music, dreamy and sensuous, came drifting out of concealed speakers. Paola began to dance to it, her body fluid and graceful under the clinging dress, her eyes half closed, and a little secret smile playing around her lips.

A minute or two later Carlo invited Bianca to dance with him and they joined Paola. And the next thing, Alix supposed, would be that Liam would join in too, and that was something she would prefer not to watch.

She swallowed the remainder of her coffee, and picking up her brandy goblet, slipped through the curtains and out on to the terrace. There was no moon, but the stars looked like diamonds sprinkled across velvet. The air was warm and full of scents and silence. She leaned on the stone balustrade, letting the peace and beauty of the evening soothe some of the ache inside her.

From just behind her, Liam said, 'If you're considering wandering farther afield tonight, then think again.

Carlo takes all this security very seriously, and he has men with dogs patrolling the grounds.'

She started. The sound of his voice was the first hint she had had of his approach.

Without turning, she said, 'Thank you for the warning.'

'It isn't the only one I have for you.' He paused. 'I wouldn't become too friendly with Paola Minozza, if I were you.'

There was a brief hectic silence, then she said chokingly, 'Why? Because you might find it inconvenient.'

His brows lifted slightly. 'I'm not sure exactly how I feature in all this, but let it pass. I'm only warning you, because you could be heading for a major clash with Bianca. But perhaps that's what you want.'

'It's not what I want.' She got that little flare of temper back under control again, but he had come to lean on the balustrade beside her, his sleeve almost brushing hers, and her senses were jumping again at his proximity. 'And Bianca doesn't interfere in my friendships.'

'I had the definite impression that she interfered at almost every level in your life,' he said coolly. 'When I saw you this afternoon, I thought you'd begun to fight back—begun to live as a woman in your own right, instead of a cipher in her shadow, but you soon disabused me of that notion. But believe me, Alix, if you start aligning yourself with Paola, then even dressing in a sack and putting a bag over your head won't save you from Bianca's wrath.'

She said, 'I don't understand one word of all this. Why should she object? Carlo wants us to be friends, after all . . .'

'Carlo isn't only a great director, he also has an inbuilt sense of mischief which sometimes gets the better of him.' Liam's voice was crisp. 'If you haven't worked out for yourself what's going on, then I suggest you ask Leon Farnaby. By the look of him, realisation has just dawned, and he's trying to come to terms with it through a haze of alcohol.'

That was something she could not deny. Leon's behaviour had been worrying her all evening.

'I'll go and find him,' she began, half turning, but Liam's hand descended on her arm.

'It will have to wait until tomorrow. He's gone to bed,' he said with dry amusement, and Alix guessed that Leon had probably been dismissed like a naughty child.

'I'd better go in anyway,' she muttered, trying unavailingly to free herself from his grasp.

'Why?' he enquired mockingly. 'Surely you can't be cold?'

'Hardly,' she said shortly, glad that the darkness masked the sudden colour which had invaded her face at this deliberately ambiguous question.

'Then what are you afraid of?' he asked softly.

'Do I have to be afraid?' she said tautly. 'Is it so impossible that I might just not want to be alone with you?'

'I'd say possible, but unlikely.' He still sounded amused. 'Stop fluttering, secretary bird. You'll only hurt yourself.'

But I could cope with that, she thought. Self-inflicted wounds would heal, but the hurt you could do me might make me bleed slowly for the rest of my life.

She took a breath. 'You warned me just now about making Bianca angry,' she said levelly. 'Perhaps I ought to extend the same warning to you.'

'It isn't necessary,' he said. 'She doesn't own me. No one does.'

'I'm sure of that,' she said. 'Nevertheless she does have—let's say, a short-term lease, and she'll expect her money's worth.'

The silence between them almost crackled, then he said tightly, 'You little bitch.'

The anger in his voice made her flinch, but at least he was no longer holding her. She was free—yet she had never felt more captive. She was filled with an over-whelming urge to throw herself into his arms, to feel the hard pressure of his body against hers, and the move-ment of his mouth against her skin.

But the time for that was past, she thought. There was a barrier between them now which she had built quite deliberately of her own free will. She had flicked Liam on the raw, and even if she went into his arms, he wouldn't want her there. Not now. Not ever again, she thought.

There was an ache in her throat, and a stinging behind her eyelids. She was close to tears, she recognised with panic. Her only wish was to sink down on the flags of the terrace, lean her forehead against the cold stone of the balustrade and weep her heartache away. But that was impossible.

Moving like an automaton, she moved back across the terrace to the lighted windows of the *salotto*. Inside the room, the music still played, and now Carlo was dancing with Paola. Alix's eyes flickered apprehensively to where Bianca was standing, her hand clasped so rigidly round the glass she was holding that her knuckles showed white.

She was watching Paola, watching her dance round Carlo like some fragile white moth in her flimsy dress, and because she thought she was unobserved there was a look in her eyes which made Alix feel she had intruded upon a nightmare.

She felt herself recoil and gasped as she collided with Liam, who had entered the room just behind her.

He gave her a long steady look, and then, his mouth curling in a mixture of contempt and distaste, he took her by the shoulders and put her away from him.

She watched him walk away across the room to Bianca's side, saw him smile, take her hand, draw her into his arms and begin to move to the music, their bodies swaying together in sinuous unison. She saw Bianca throw her head back, her mouth pouting seductively as she looked up into the dark face above her, her arms lifting to entwine round his neck.

Alix felt her jaw clench with tension. Bianca had made her angry before, she had aggravated her, hurt her and humiliated her on occasion, but she had never before made her so blazingly, passionately jealous that she wanted to fly at her, dragging her nails down her face. The intensity of her emotions frightened her, and she knew she had to get out of the room and escape before they overwhelmed her. She began to edge round towards the door, almost flattening herself against the wall, scarcely daring to breathe in case any of them looked at her and saw what she was no longer sure she could hide.

Outside in the dimly lit hall, she stopped and released her pent-up breath in one long shuddering sigh. She had gained a temporary respite, that was all.

There was no escape, no freedom, and never could be. Some lines from a half-remembered poem came beating at her brain. 'While I am I,' she thought, 'and you are you. So long as the world contains us both . . .'

And felt the first scalding tear scar its way down the curve of her cheek.

CHAPTER SIX

PLANS, she thought, a long time—a lifetime—later, as she sat at the dressing table in her room, brushing her hair. That was what she had to make. She had to give her future some serious consideration. She could not go on as she had been doing, that was certain.

Another job—that had to be the first priority. Perhaps Carlo Veronese could help. He had contacts everywhere, not merely in the film world. Maybe she would stay in Italy—even work in Venice. It wasn't what she had visualised, but then very little ever was.

She had not foreseen the devastating effect Liam Brant would have on her life. She still could not assimilate totally what had happened to her. She felt as if she had woken one day to see a small black cloud on the edge of her tranquil horizon, only to see it swell and grow into a hurricane, sweeping through her life, destroying any cosy preconceptions she might have had about the relationships between men and women.

She had never regarded herself as being in any way frigid. She enjoyed being held and kissed, and she had never doubted for a moment that when she gave herself in the ultimate surrender it would be with joy and passion. But none of the young men who had touched and kissed her had ever filled her with the craving which Liam could evoke by the merest brush of his hand or mouth.

It was madness, she thought, putting down her brush and staring at the pale large-eyed reflection in the mirror. She knew so little about him, their paths had barely crossed, and yet she could hardly draw breath without thinking about him. Without wanting him, she acknowledged raggedly.

She thought of Peter, struggling to bring him to mind, as she might last night's dream. She had enjoyed his company, the theatres and the dinners, and the slow building of rapport. She had thought she had known heartache over his desertion, but what had she known?

The memory of Bianca in Liam's arms, smiling up at him, stabbed her with knives. This was why she had tried so hard to avoid him during his visits to the house in London. She had been wary then, standing sentinel over her senses and emotions. But that afternoon, beside the pool, one unguarded moment had been her downfall.

Bianca would not be pleased when she told her she was leaving, she thought detachedly, but she would not allow her to talk her out of it as she had done last time.

I wish I'd gone then, she thought. If I'd stuck to my guns and left, at least I would have been spared this.

But if I had, the thought struggled to escape from beneath the weariness and misery in her mind, then I would never have known what it was like to be in his arms. And I would have been half alive for the rest of my life.

The knock on the door brought her sharply out of her abstraction. She swivelled round on the stool and stared at the door, aware that her heart was thudding. Her unknown visitor was pushing at the door now, rattling the handle, but there had been a key in the door and Alix had used it.

'Who is it?'

'Who the hell do you think it is?' Bianca's voice.

Alix sighed. The door gave another rattle. 'Hurry up and let me in!' The edge was sharpening in Bianca's voice.

'I was just going to bed,' Alix protested as she opened the door and Bianca pushed past her into the room. It wasn't true. She'd been doing everything except going to bed. She'd wept, and dried her eyes, and cleansed her face at least twice, and had a bath, and walked a mile up and down the room.

'I want to talk to you.' Bianca also had changed for the night. Her nightdress and matching peignoir were in orchid pink chiffon, trimmed with lace. Alix stared at her in amazement.

'I'm sorry,' she said, 'I didn't get your message.'

'I didn't send one,' Bianca interrupted petulantly. 'Monty's in my suite, fussing about my clothes, with one of the maids and the housekeeper. It's like Grand Central Station in there, and I wanted to speak to you privately.' She walked over to the dressing table, and stood looking down at the small array of cosmetics, touching a scent bottle with one pink-tipped finger as if she hardly recognised what it was. 'Did you know Liam Brant was going to be here?' she said abruptly.

Alix leaned against the door, trying to absorb some of the strength of its sturdy panels. 'No, I didn't,' she returned levelly. 'Why do you ask?'

Bianca turned her head and looked at her for a long, silent moment.

'He isn't for you,' she said.

'I never thought he was.' That at least was the truth, she thought.

'Didn't you? That wasn't the impression you gave this afternoon.' Bianca's lips twisted in the semblance of a smile. 'My rooms overlook the pool area.'

Alix went cold. 'I see.'

'I don't think so.' Alix realised, amazed, that Bianca was not enjoying this. Her eyes were sober, almost troubled. 'You're such a child, Alix. You can't afford to get involved with a man like that. He'd break you into small pieces and throw you away.'

'Does it matter?' Alix stared down at the floor.

'Oh, for God's sake, don't make all the mistakes that I made.' Bianca went over to the window, and pulled back the curtain with an impatient hand. 'I should have left you in your little suburb, with Margaret and Philip and the other girl—what's her name?'

'Debbie,' Alix said quietly. 'Why didn't you?'

She'd never asked before. She'd always taken it for granted that it was just a piece of good fortune, that sudden, unexpected visit, and later the offer of a job, prompted, she'd always thought, by Lester Marchant. Bianca had needed a secretary, and remembered that she had a niece who planned to be one.

But now it didn't seem so simple. When Bianca had set out before to take a man Alix wanted, whether for a light flirtation or a full-blooded affair, she had never bothered to offer any kind of excuse or reason. But that was what she appeared to be doing now, and Alix wondered why.

Bianca shrugged, letting the curtain fall back into place. 'Let's just say it seemed like a good idea at the time.' She turned fully, extending her hands in a curiously appealing gesture. 'Alix, believe me when I say I've known men like Liam Brant before. I met the first when I wasn't much older than you—single-minded, obsessively ambitious. Nothing else mattered. I can see that now, but I couldn't see it then. I thought that I mattered, but I was wrong, and I found out the hard way.'

'Bianca, please.' Alix was embarrassed. 'You don't have to justify yourself to me.'

Bianca's hands dropped to her sides. 'Is that what I'm doing? Perhaps you're right. I thought I was trying to warn you.'

'I don't need to be warned. You said I was a child, but I'd already worked out for myself that Liam was out of my league,' Alix said through stiff lips. 'If it matters, whatever you saw at the pool wasn't serious.'

'Not on his side, perhaps,' Bianca said harshly. 'But you, darling, give yourself away every time you look at him, or didn't you realise?' She stopped, and put her hand to her mouth. 'Alix, I'm sorry. I didn't mean that as it sounded. It's just that I've always had this irresistible attraction to bastards, and I don't want you to inherit it.' She gave a little shaky laugh. 'Absurd, isn't it?'

Absurd, and frightening at the same time. Alix felt dazed. Bianca had never spoken to her like this before, never treated her with such intimacy, and she was unsure how to respond. Bianca had set her at a distance when she first went to work for her by insisting that she was a cousin instead of a niece, and she had never made the least effort to treat Alix any more warmly because of the relationship between them. It was Monty who had always shared the intimacy—whatever inner counsels that Bianca permitted.

And yet here they were, two women talking in the night about a man they both wanted, fumbling their way towards some strange kind of understanding.

What's happening? she thought.

She said, 'I expect I take after my mother. She loved a lovely man. And you married Lester. He wasn't a bastard.'

She wished she hadn't mentioned him, because Bianca looked stricken suddenly. In spite of the gorgeous negligee, the coiled black hair, and the colour on her cheeks and lips and eyes which she always wore, even in bed, for that moment she looked her age, and vulnerable with it.

Bianca took a breath, and the moment passed. She was herself again, vibrant and glamorous, even smiling a little.

She said, 'No, he wasn't. Probably that's why I treated him so badly. I should have hung on to him, Alix. He was one of the best things that ever happened.' The skirts of her negligee whispered across the tiled floor as she came towards the door. She lifted a hand and touched Alix's cheek. Her fingers felt cold. She said, 'Don't hate me, Alix,' and went.

Alix made her way over to the bed, and sank down on the edge of it. Clever, she thought, clever. Any time over the past years she could have hated Bianca. There had been times when hurt and resentment had threatened to take over. She still had to get away—that hadn't

changed—but she wouldn't leave in bitterness. Tonight
a corner of the veil which hid the real Bianca Layton
from the world had been lifted, and it had left Alix
shaken. She didn't really think what she felt was pity. It
was more subtle than that, and certainly less explicable.

There was no need for her to feel sorry for Bianca—
to feel anything for Bianca. Bianca was a winner, or at
any rate leading the survivors. The middle-aged woman
who had briefly looked out of her face tonight would be
shut away again, and only Alix would guess that she
existed.

Liam Brant would never see that other woman, she
thought. He wouldn't look past the façade of beauty,
the aura of glamour, any more than any of Bianca's
other lovers had been allowed to do.

The word 'lover' went through her like a lance. Her
hand went to her throat, tugging free the bow which
fastened her housecoat as if she were choking.

There's no air in the room, she thought. That's why I
can't breathe. She parted the curtains, and opened the
doors leading to the balcony, propping them slightly
ajar. For a moment she stood there, breathing deeply,
filling herself with the warm scents of the night air. It
was very still, but not totally peaceful because below
her in the barely seen paths and hedges of the formal
sunken garden, she could just discern movement.

One of Carlo's security men, she thought, accompanied by savage dog, riding shotgun on us all.

She stepped back into her room. It was a weird,
twisted world she had been adopted into, and she would
bid it farewell without a trace of regret.

But there would be so much else that she would be
unable to dismiss so easily, she thought, as she climbed
into bed and pulled the covers round her as if they were
a shield.

She was still asleep the following morning when Monty
knocked on the door.

'She's having breakfast in bed,' Monty announced abruptly. 'She says you can amuse yourself this morning, but she'll see you in the suite after lunch.' She gave Alix a narrow-eyed look. 'Perhaps you'd better stay in bed yourself. What's the matter with you?'

'Perhaps the flight took more out of me than I thought,' Alix shrugged.

'Oh?' Monty didn't sound convinced. 'That man's here, as I suppose you know. I suppose you have to give him ten out of ten for sheer persistence. This book must mean a lot to him.'

'It must,' Alix agreed, relieved to find her voice sound so normal.

Monty's brow was furrowed. 'And this girl Paola Minozza. What do you know about her?'

'Very little,' Alix said carefully. 'Just that she's a cousin of Carlo Veronese. And a girlfriend of Liam Brant's.'

Monty nodded. 'As long as that's all she is,' she said cryptically, and took her leave.

Alix showered and dressed, donning brief denim shorts and a matching halternecked sun-top, shaped like a tiny waistcoat, in case Paola's invitation to play tennis was renewed. She also took one of her own bikinis out of a drawer. It was black, and although by no means old-fashioned, considerably more circumspect than the one she had borrowed the previous day.

If there was no tennis, she would swim and laze by the pool, she thought. And as soon as she got the chance, she would talk to Carlo Veronese about helping her to find another job.

Breakfast was being served on the terrace, she discovered when she got downstairs. Giovanni was collecting used dishes and cutlery when she arrived, and only Leon was at the table. Alix asked for orange juice, coffee and hot rolls, and as Giovanni bustled away to fetch them, gave Leon a long look.

He avoided her gaze, sipping his black coffee. 'I feel terrible,' he muttered.

'I'm not surprised,' Alix said frankly. 'Whatever got into you last night—apart from several pints of gin, that is?'

Leon looked around almost evasively. 'We can't talk here.'

'Oh, for heaven's sake,' she said sharply. 'Carlo may be security-conscious, but I doubt if he has his breakfast table bugged, and there's certainly no one within earshot. Is it something to do with Paola Minozza?'

Leon nodded jerkily, producing a handkerchief from his conventional blazer pocket and dabbing his forehead with it.

'You're worried because Liam Brant is here, and Bianca wants him, only Paola's his girl-friend, and there's going to be trouble, right?' Alix asked, trying to make bricks with what little straw seemed available.

Leon's eyes swivelled towards her sharply in a movement which clearly hurt. 'What on earth are you talking about? Are you mad? What the hell's Liam Brant got to do with all this—except that he'll be in a ringside seat making notes for this bloody book, in a perfect position to record the whole mess for posterity?'

'Then what . . .'

Leon gave her an irritated look. 'Paola's Carlo's woman. Surely you weren't taken in by all that nonsense about cousins? You can be incredibly naïve, Alix.'

'That is so true,' she said. 'Then what's the problem?'

Leon spread his hands wide. 'You've seen her, haven't you? What do you think?'

'I think she's incredibly beautiful,' Alix said honestly.

'Oh, she's that all right.' Leon made it sound like an insult. He gestured at the sky. 'I swear I never saw it coming. But Bianca will never believe it, although I warned her that Veronese was a tricky blighter.'

'Not more dark warnings!' Alix groaned. 'They're coming at me from all sides.'

'Then I hope you take more notice of them than Bianca does,' Leon said petulantly.

'Try me and see,' she invited. 'Tell me about Paola Minozza before I pour that coffee you're not drinking over your head.'

Leon sat for a moment, staring in front of him, then he said slowly, 'Suppose I told you that Carlo met her at a studio in Rome where she was doing a film test—a very successful one. Could you put two and two together then?'

Alix thought—Francesca—my God, he means that Paola is going to play Francesca in the film, and not Bianca.

Aloud, she said, 'It can't be true! She's pinning everything on this film.'

Leon looked glum. 'Oh, she's being offered a part in it,' he said heavily. 'But not the lead. Carlo broke the news to me when we arrived yesterday. He got Bianca here to talk her into it because he knew that if he just made the offer through me, she'd turn him down.' He swallowed. 'Paola is going to play Francesca, but even if she doesn't, he told me that it isn't going to be offered to Bianca. He was brutally frank. He said that the view is she's too old—that there's a generation who know she can't possibly be the age she's supposed to be in the film, and that not even a star of her magnitude could hope to get away with it for ever.'

Giovanni arrived smiling with the food, but Alix's appetite had deserted her. She poured herself some black coffee and drank quickly.

At last she said, 'What part for her does he have in mind?'

'Would you believe—Francesca's mother,' Leon said unhappily, and they exchanged an appalled glance.

Alix said, 'She must never know. You'll have to think of something to get her back to London before Carlo says anything. We can't let this happen to her.'

'It's bound to happen sooner or later.' Leon stirred.

'Can I have some of your coffee? This is cold and quite revolting.' He paused. 'I don't suppose you've been aware of it, Alix, but Bianca isn't getting the offers she used to. Some important scripts have passed her by recently, and I suspect for this very reason—that people are counting on their fingers and reckoning up exactly how long she's been around, even before she was at the top. It's no reflection on her acting talents, or her ability to get them to the box office. It's just that you have to be young to get anywhere these days. Bianca may look ageless, but it's occurring to people who matter in the industry that she isn't. That she can't be. It's as simple as that.'

Alix said heatedly, 'That's horrible!'

'It's life,' Leon retorted. He sighed heavily. 'What makes it worse is that she actually was being considered for the role of Francesca at the beginning. Then the guys putting up the finance intervened.' He grimaced. 'It seems that Lester Marchant is among them.'

'Oh, no!' Alix was appalled. 'He couldn't. He isn't like that.'

Leon looked at her shrewdly. 'Perhaps he wasn't, but people change. And Bianca gave him a pretty acrimonious divorce. He could have seen this as a way of getting his revenge. There's an old show business saying—be nice to people on the way up, because you may need them on the way down. Bianca may well be wishing in a few years that she'd paid it some attention.'

He drank the coffee she poured for him, and pushed back his chair.

'I'm going to phone Seb—to make sure he continues to keep the Press at bay. If Bianca takes the other role, then I want any stories that appear to be positive ones—that her career is taking a new path—more mature roles, that sort of thing. But first we have to persuade her, and it's not going to be easy.' He glanced around him wryly. 'Perhaps she'll melt under the hot Italian sun.'

When she was alone, Alix took one of the rolls and

broke it, spreading it with some of the jam provided in a cut-glass bowl, warm and rich with the taste of apricots.

She felt too tense to be hungry, but she needed the food and forced herself to make the effort.

She tried to imagine what Bianca's reaction would be when she discovered what Carlo Veronese had in mind, but it was beyond her. She supposed that Leon was right to be apprehensive. Normally he was second to none in assessing the possibilities of the films Bianca worked in, but this time he had slipped up badly, and if she lashed out when the truth became known, he would probably be the principal target.

Other film actresses resigned themselves to the passage of time, and if they suffered traumas in doing so, then they suffered them in private. But Alix had little hope that Bianca would follow an equally dignified path. It made her shudder to think how explosive her reaction could be to even a hint that her days as a leading lady were behind her. Bianca regarded herself as a star, and would probably always do so. The role of supporting actress would have no appeal whatsoever.

A shadow fell across the breakfast table, and she looked up with a little start.

Liam stood, looking down at her, his brows sardonically raised as he assimilated the brevity of her shorts and top. Alix felt the burning betraying colour rise in her face.

She said hurriedly, aware of a husky note in her voice that she couldn't control, 'Would you like some coffee?'

'No.' His eyes moved from the slender tanned length of her legs, to the shadowed valley between her breasts, revealed by the deeply slashed neckline of the denim waistcoat. 'What else is on offer?'

'Nothing,' she said shortly, hating herself for blushing. She pushed her chair back, and made to rise. 'I—I must go.'

His fingers captured her wrist, halting her. 'Where are you off to in such a hurry?'

'I do have a job. Bianca may want me and...'

'Bianca doesn't need you until this afternoon, and don't pretend you didn't get the message,' he said. 'I'm going to do a preliminary interview with her about her early life, for the book, and although I'm using a tape recorder, she wants you there to take a full note of everything that's said.'

Alix heard this with dismay. 'But surely a tape recording...' she began.

He shrugged. 'Argue with Bianca, not me, secretary bird. Having a child among us taking notes isn't a prospect I view with any enthusiasm either. Apparently Bianca feels a tape can be doctored.'

'In other words, she doesn't trust you.' Alix stared back at him, her eyes shadowed. 'Your irresistible charm must be on the wane.'

'Is that a fact?' His voice was cool, but she could hear the anger simmering below the surface. 'Don't push too hard, Alix, or I could still be tempted to prove you wrong. Your resistance hasn't been exactly infallible.'

'Up to now, perhaps.' She made herself speak calmly. 'You don't have to remind me, Liam. I'm sufficiently ashamed of myself already.'

'That isn't quite the reaction I had in mind.'

'Nevertheless, it's the only one there is,' she said. 'Please let go of me.'

'That isn't what you want,' he said, and his fingers moved gently in a circle on the inside of her wrist as if he was testing for himself the tremulousness of her pulse.

'But it's what I mean,' she said between her teeth, and tore herself free. 'Arrogant men are not in my line, Mr Brant, however well versed in sexual expertise. I prefer people who care.'

'Like Peter Barnet, I suppose,' he said bitingly.

'Do you really think you're so superior?' She was trembling suddenly.

'Yes, I do think so. Peter's a fool, and always was—

snatching at shadows, when he could have had the substance.'

'You damned hypocrite!' she whispered fiercely. 'God—is it any wonder Bianca doesn't trust you?'

For one agonising moment his eyes, dark and glittering, bored into hers. She could sense the violence in him and flinched as if a blow had actually been struck.

'Don't look like that,' he ordered roughly. 'I've never hit a woman yet, and I'm not starting with you, Alix, even though you deserve it. There are other, better ways of punishing you, as you'll find out.'

He turned and walked away, and Alix watched him go, seeing the glitter of the sunlight dissolve into a thousand shimmering sparks as she fought back her tears.

She went down the terrace steps, and paused at the bottom, looking round almost blindly, wondering which way to go. She needed to be on her own to regain her equilibrium, so she avoided the swimming pool area. She wandered along a dusty path lined on both sides with tall flowering shrubs, turned a corner, and found herself in the formal garden she could see from her window.

The warmth of the morning sun was like a comforting arm thrown across her shoulders as she moved down the paved walks. Around her, among the flowers, she could hear the contented hum of bees, and gradually a kind of peace began to fill her.

She found she was thinking about her mother, and the garden she tended at home with such anxious pride. Alix wished she had taken more interest in it, and helped more. At least then she would have been able to identify some of the plants and shrubs in the precisely patterned beds. All the paths led to a circular paved area, set with stone benches, and in the absolute centre an ancient sundial, the pedestal carved into the shape of a smiling faun. There was lettering carved into the stone around the dial, and Alix traced it with her finger, removing fragments of lichen with her nail.

Her mouth twisted wryly as she translated the words 'Remember only the hours that are serene.' Could that ever really be possible? she wondered sadly. In the years ahead, would she look back on these days under the Italian sun, and recall only the wild happiness which had surged through her when Liam held her in his arms? Or would she remember how she had paid for every kiss, every caress, and if his warning was to be believed, would continue to pay?

She shivered in spite of the heat, closing her eyes for a moment, then started a little as she heard someone call her name. She looked round and saw Paola walking towards her.

She was wearing a cream cheesecloth tunic over a bikini, and her hair gleamed in the sunshine.

'*Buon giorno,* Alix! Did you sleep well? I've been looking for you. I thought you might be here. It is a romantic place, and you, I think, are a romantic person.'

Alix returned her smile, shaking her head in slight confusion.

'I don't think so. If anything, I'm too prosaic.'

'I think you do yourself an injustice.' Paola looked her over. 'But not, however, this morning. You look very beautiful. You should not be walking here alone.'

'I enjoy my own company,' Alix returned defensively. 'I came here because my window overlooks this part of the grounds, and I wanted to explore it.'

Paola gave a little shrug. 'It is old, of course. Older than the house. Carlo's wife loved this garden, and persuaded him to buy the property, even though it was little better than a ruin. He built the house for her, but sadly she died not many years after it was finished.'

Alix gave her a quick glance. 'I'm sorry, I didn't know.'

'Why should you? Carlo does not often speak of it.'

'And he's never considered—remarrying?' Alix asked.

Paola's eyes twinkled. 'Do you mean—will he marry me? No, *cara*. It is not what either of us wish.'

'I didn't mean to pry,' Alix said ruefully, but Paola's expression remained friendly and smiling.

'It is natural you should be interested, as we are all living under the same roof. One would have to be a saint, probably, not to ask certain questions.'

'I lay no claim to sanctity,' Alix laughed. 'But I really hadn't the least idea. In fact I thought . . .' She stopped in some confusion as she remembered exactly what she had thought.

'If you didn't guess, then someone must have told you.' Paola gave her a mischievous look. 'I am no saint either, and I also like to ask questions, therefore I don't think it was Liam. When Carlo and I came down to the pool yesterday, I picked up certain—vibrations which led me to believe you were discussing no one but yourselves. Well, am I right?'

Alix flushed. 'Partly,' she admitted with constraint.

'And I do not think it was your aunt,' Paola continued serenely. 'Because all she is concerned with is who is going to play Francesca.'

'Why do you call Bianca my aunt?' Alix asked apprehensively.

Paola shrugged gracefully. 'Isn't that who she is? She said you were her cousin, but that's what Carlo calls me, so I assumed it was a fiction also. Yet you must be related, because you are so like her—so the obvious answer seems to be that you're her niece. Why? Is it a closely guarded secret?'

'It used to be,' Alix said with a sigh. 'Now it seems to be common knowledge. But I'm not really like her.'

'No? Haven't you seen any photographs of her when she was a young girl? Carlo was showing me some stills from some of her earliest films, and she wore her hair very much as you do now. The bone structure too is unmistakable.'

'But Bianca is beautiful,' Alix said, half to herself.

Paola's eyes widened. 'And you think you are not? Bianca has glamour, that's true, but she is no more beautiful than you are—except when you wear a hideous dress as you did last night,' she added candidly. 'I don't want to hurt your feelings, Alix, but I'm surprised she has never given you advice on how to dress.'

'Oh, but she has,' Alix said drily. 'Only not quite on the lines you seem to think. In fact she thoroughly approved of the dress I wore last night.'

For a moment Paola stared at her, then her smile widened. 'Then that proves that you are beautiful,' she said gently. 'And that she realises it too. Poor Alix, or perhaps I should say poor Bianca—to be so frightened of her own flesh and blood.'

'She has nothing to fear from me,' said Alix. 'In any way.'

'You love her,' Paola said. It was more a statement than a question.

Alix spread her hands helplessly. 'I suppose I must, although God knows there've been times when I felt I hated her. I've been all set to walk out several times—now is one of them. I don't think I can take any more, and yet in an odd way I feel she needs me.' She laughed bitterly. 'That's nonsense, of course. She has Monty. I've always had to walk on eggshells to avoid poaching on her preserves too.' She made herself smile. 'I'd like a simple job without personality problems and complications. Do you think Carlo could help me find one?'

'In the film industry?' Paola asked derisively. 'No way, *cara*. They are all lunatics. You're a person who needs to be stable, Alix. To be secure. I think you should stop thinking about other people and their needs, and start considering your own. Do you want to be married?'

The question caught Alix on the hop, and flustered her. 'Yes—no—I suppose—eventually. I haven't thought about it that much.'

'Then you should.' Paola was watching her. 'Find a

guy, fall in love with him, and spend the rest of your lives making each other happy.'

'You make it sound like bliss,' said Alix after a shaky pause.

Paola grinned. 'It probably could be. Marriage isn't for me, but I still believe in it. I'm either a fool or an idealist—probably both. Now, we've been serious long enough. Let's go and swim. It's too hot for tennis.'

As she turned, Alix said softly, 'Paola, supposing you found the man you wanted, only he didn't want you. What then?'

Paola's voice was gentle. 'Then you find someone else, *cara*. Someone who can love you as you need to be loved. Because for someone like you, nothing less will do.'

No, Alix thought achingly, as she followed the other girl out of the garden and towards the pool, nothing less would do for her.

When she had begged Liam to love her at the poolside, he had read it as an invitation to a brief sexual encounter, a satisfaction of the desires he had so deliberately aroused. That had been humiliating enough, so she could only be thankful he hadn't guessed she was offering her heart and soul, as well as her body.

That would be the painful secret she would carry within her for as long as she lived.

CHAPTER SEVEN

WHEN Alix let herself in to Bianca's suite that afternoon, it was to find the room almost in darkness. The shutters had been pulled across the windows, and Alix stood hesitating, wondering whether Bianca who had lunched in her suite was asleep on one of the sofas, and if she should return later.

As she stood, peering through the gloom, she sensed a movement, and said, 'Bianca?'

'No,' Liam answered, and began to open the shutters. He had been missing most of the morning, and had not joined the party in the dining room for lunch. Perhaps that meant that he had been here with Bianca all the time, Alix thought.

She said hurriedly, 'Is Bianca resting? I'll come back in half an hour and . . .'

'I've no idea what she's doing,' said Liam with something of a snap. 'I only got here moments before you did. However, run away if you want to.' He wrenched at the shutter, folding it back into place, and sunlight spilled into the room.

Alix felt selfconscious standing in the middle of the room clutching her notebook and a supply of sharpened pencils, and she moved over to a small writing desk in one corner. She put the book down, and arranged her pencils meticulously beside it, then opened one of the drawers in the desk at random as if she was looking for something. It was only a ploy—an attempt to look busy so that she would not have to look at Liam or talk to him—but it was a total failure, because the drawer was empty. With a little furious grimace, she tried to push it shut, but the desk was old and the drawer jammed.

'Oh hell!' Alix muttered under her breath.

'Here, let me.' Liam sounded exasperated. His hands descended on her shoulders, moving her out of the way. He removed the drawer, examined it, his fingers exploring the wood for snags, then fitted it back deftly, and without the slightest trouble.

He stood back and looked at the desk. 'You shouldn't lose your temper with a piece as nice as this,' he commented.

'I did not lose my temper,' Alix contradicted, her teeth almost grinding as she considered the contrariness of inanimate objects.

'Then I'd hate to be around when you do,' he said sardonically. He looked her over, absorbing the crisp lines of the button-through denim skirt, and the white shirt blouse with the sleeves rolled back to the elbow.

'Very neat,' he said. 'But I prefer the gear you had on this morning.'

'I don't dress to please you,' Alix said tautly. 'And I am sick and tired of this constant stream of comment about everything I wear.' She snatched up one of her pencils as if to examine the point, and snapped it. 'Oh blast!' she exploded. 'Now look what you've made me do!'

'Just a minute.' Inexorably he turned her to face him, his eyes searching her face. 'I haven't made you do anything. You've been like a cat on hot bricks ever since you entered this room. Calm down, or do you want Bianca to see you like this?'

'Leave me alone,' she pleaded raggedly, and heard him laugh huskily deep in his throat.

'Do you think I don't wish I could? Oh God, Alix!' He pulled her roughly into his arms and his mouth came down on hers, hard and forceful, shocking her into an uncontrolled and total response. She pressed her body against his as if she was attempting to be absorbed into his bloodstream, her lips parting beneath the onslaught of his kiss. His hands were moving almost convulsively against her shoulderblades, drawing her closer.

In some dim recess of her mind, she was aware how much she was betraying by her eager surrender, but it no longer seemed to matter. In whatever wilderness awaited her, she would cherish these moments when Liam kissed her as if she was his woman, as if this passionate joining of their mouths, this sweet invasion was only a preliminary to the pleasure to come.

His hands were on her skin now, moving gently but surely, bringing every nerve ending to singing life. Little sparks seemed to be exploding behind her closed eyelids, and she heard a whimper burst from her throat as his fingers cupped her breast, his thumb stroking caressingly across the sensitive dusky tip. She was dizzy with desire for him, her body one sweet sensuous ache of longing.

His mouth left hers to travel down her throat, lingering to press kisses on her pulse, then take a leisurely trail to where the prim white collar of the blouse halted any further progress. He gave a short unsteady laugh, and said, his voice muffled against her skin, 'Unfasten it.'

That was how it had begun, she recalled as if she was in a dream. An unfastened button had been the start of her beguilement. Only, she hadn't known it then, although she'd scented danger. Her only thought had been to keep him away from Bianca . . .

Bianca! The dream was over, and she was struggling suddenly, trying to push him away, swaying as she fought to keep her balance.

'What's the matter?' Liam stared down at her, a faint flush along his cheekbones, his eyes glittering.

'Oh, nothing,' she said bitterly. At any moment the door which led to the bedroom could have opened and Bianca could have seen them, she thought with shame. She turned away catching a painful glimpse of herself in an ornate gilt-framed mirror on one of the walls. Her hair was dishevelled, the once neat blouse hung tipsily over the waistband of her skirt, and her mouth looked blurred and swollen.

'Oh God,' she said savagely, raking at her hair with shaking fingers, then trying to force her recalcitrant blouse back into her skirt.

'You'll tear it if you aren't careful.' He actually sounded almost amused. 'Let me . . .'

'You won't touch me.' She could hear sounds of movement from the inner room, so kept her voice low. 'You'll never touch me again, do you hear? I must have been mad!'

'No,' he said. 'Not mad, only too human. She's still there, isn't she, Alix—that vibrant, passionate girl I saw on the stairs that day—and occasionally she escapes from behind that Puritanical shield you've built round her—God only knows why.'

'Perhaps to keep her safe from—from womanisers like you. What are you looking for, Liam? More sensational copy for your next book? "Aunt and niece—I had them both," by an expert.'

'You little bitch,' he said slowly. 'If I thought you meant that I'd shake you until your teeth rattled.'

'Well, I do mean it.' She risked another look in the mirror, and saw with relief that she seemed to have reverted to an approximation of her usual neatness. She could only hope that Bianca wouldn't look too closely at her. 'I'm here to work, and I don't regard being pawed by you as a bonus. Is that understood?'

There was a brief silence, and she waited through it, her teeth sunk painfully in her lower lip, terrified that he might carry out his threat, because she knew that if he touched her again, even in anger, she would break into tiny pieces.

When he spoke his voice was clipped. 'Clearly understood. But if you're waiting for me to apologise, you'll wait for ever.'

Alix moved her shoulders wearily. 'I don't want an apology. It was my fault too.'

'My God, what an admission,' he mocked. 'You actually have feelings. Break out of your self-imposed chrysalis before it's too late, Alix. You might even enjoy being a woman.'

Feeling defeated, she walked over to the desk and sank down on the chair, glad of its support. She opened her pad and wrote the date, amazed to find it was even legible.

'Darlings!' Bianca said gaily from her bedroom doorway. 'Have I kept you waiting? I'm so sorry.'

She was wearing a black silk caftan, embroidered in panels down the front with a myriad tiny flowers in pastel colour, and her dark hair was piled on top of her head, and secured by a circlet of matching flowers. It was what she called her geisha look, and it gave her an incredibly fragile appearance. In one hand she was clutching a thick bundle of typescript, which Alix eyed with misgiving.

'Yes,' Bianca nodded at her. 'Carlo sent me the amended script along this morning. It's marvellous—miraculous! I can't wait for everything to be settled. It will be the best thing I've ever done—wait and see.'

Alix felt sick. She couldn't look at Bianca suddenly, turning away to fiddle with her pad. She felt she hated Carlo Veronese. This was a piece of calculated cruelty, inviting her here like this—making her think the role was as good as hers when all the time . . .

And this was why Liam was here, she thought bitterly. It wasn't a biography he was going to write, but an obituary. The final disintegration of a great star, the end of a legend. Bianca was programmed to self-destruction and he wouldn't lift a finger to stop her. He might be sleeping with her, but there was no love, no respect for her in him, or he couldn't let it happen.

Bianca was seating herself on a chaise-longue, fussing with the cushions, while Liam made some last-minute adjustments to his recorder.

She said, 'You know what I want, Alix—a full note of everything that's said—just to keep the record straight.' She smiled charmingly at Liam, crossing her legs, smoothing down the folds of the caftan. 'Not that I anticipate any problems,' she added softly, her tone teasing and intimate.

Alix wanted to scream. She stared rigidly down at the page of her book until the symbols blurred.

'Then we'll make a start,' Liam said calmly.

As the interview progressed Alix had to admit albeit unwillingly that he knew his job. He was getting Bianca to talk about her early days on the stage, her first job as an assistant stage manager in rep, drawing anecdotes out of her that Alix could swear she'd forgotten until that moment—like the leading man who had obstinately worn his wig backwards for an entire fortnight's run of a Jacobean tragedy because he had disagreed with the producer's interpretation of the play, and the ageing actress who had substituted neat gin for the carafe of water she was supposed to sip from, and had been legless before the third act even began. She was animated and laughing as she reminisced, Liam encouraging her by an occasional question, sometimes just a word or an inflection.

Alix was covering pages of her notebook, but although her hand was beginning to ache, she didn't want to ask for a break. She was too fascinated by the glimpse of the girl Bianca had been, doing the myriad tasks that were needed in a small impecunious repertory company, begging props from a reluctant antique shop owner, who always tried to pinch her bottom, having to fight for the chance of playing a maid occasionally, or a small character part.

She had had to fight when she started, Alix thought, oddly moved. There was no overnight success. She had always fought, only now the battle was over and she didn't know it yet.

Her eyes filled with sudden tears and she drove her pencil into the page so hard that the point broke.

Liam said sharply, 'Alix—what is it?'

'It's nothing.' She licked a scalding salt tear from the

side of her mouth. 'I—I have a bit of a headache. Too much sun this morning, I expect. I'm sorry.'

'You're as white as a sheet!' Bianca came over in a rustle of silk and leaned over her. Alix could smell the subtle fragrance of Calèche emanating from her clothes and hair, and had to fight an impulse to turn and put her head against Bianca and weep all down that beautiful caftan. 'We'll call it a day. If you feel better after dinner, you could type what there is so far, but only if you're sure you're well enough.' She turned her head. 'Liam darling, see that she gets to her room will you.'

'No—really,' Alix managed as she got to her feet. She picked up her notebook and headed for the door, but when she got into the corridor, she found Liam was beside her. 'I tell you I'm all right! I don't need you.'

'I think we've already established that,' he said, his eyes cold. 'I'm here to make sure you get to your room without collapsing, and making me feel a bigger bastard than I do already.'

'It's nothing to do with you—with what happened,' she said in a low voice.

'No?' He glanced at her. 'Then what is it? I don't fall for the "too much sun" routine.'

'It's just so awful!' she burst out. 'Listening to her—seeing her so happy—looking forward to the film—when all the time . . .'

'So you know?'

'Of course I do! Leon told me. Everyone knows except Bianca, that's what's so awful.' She ended on a little sob.

Liam said almost gently, 'Perhaps it isn't as bad—as cruel as you think.'

'Oh, I know Carlo Veronese is a friend of yours. You'd be bound to support him. He should never have got her to come here. He should have told Leon in London that she wasn't going to get the part. Doing it this way is a calculated insult, and she doesn't deserve it.'

'Don't let your loyalty run away with you, Alix,' he said drily. 'Bianca has handed it out to producers, directors, fellow-actors, husbands, lovers—even secretaries. She has to be able to take it too. Just don't go spilling the beans to her out of a mistaken sense of kindness. It may well turn out better than you think.'

'For you, undoubtedly,' she said wretchedly. 'Do you have a camera too? Her face when she hears the news will probably be the picture of the century.'

There was a long taut silence, then he said, 'My God, you have an amazing opinion of me! You sound as if you imagine I set this whole thing up, just to sell a few more copies.'

'Didn't you?' she bit at him.

'No, I didn't.' His response was fierce and immediate. 'The book's going to be a bestseller anyway. I don't need to manufacture situations. Enough exist already. Her relations with your side of the family for starters. Why won't she talk about that? I've tried half a dozen times already to get her to talk about her childhood, and it's like running into a brick wall. Why?'

'You're not trapping me into giving information that she wants to withhold,' said Alix. 'But as a matter of fact, I don't know either.'

'How did you start working for her?' he asked. 'I'm entitled to ask that, perhaps.'

'It's no secret. She needed a new secretary—and we'd met—and I think Lester persuaded her to give me a trial.' Her face warmed as she thought of him.

'You liked Lester Marchant—liked him better than the others?'

'I didn't meet the others,' she said without thinking, then scowled. 'Yes, I did like Lester. He was a warm, lovely man, and we got on well together.'

'Then you'll no doubt be surprised to hear that it was Lester who applied the pressure to ensure that Bianca didn't play Francesca,' he said.

'No,' she said. 'Someone else told me the same thing,

but I don't believe it. He wouldn't do such a thing.'

'No? You'd better ask him yourself. He'll be here in a few days.' His voice was angry. 'He's a very lucky man. You gave him the benefit of the doubt immediately.'

'He knows Bianca's here?' Alix was incredulous.

'I believe Carlo's invitation to her was his idea.'

'It just isn't possible. He loved her. You couldn't do a thing like that to someone you loved.'

'Stirring words,' he drawled. 'I may remind you of them one day.'

She brushed his words aside, frowning distractedly. 'I must tell her—warn her.'

'You won't do anything of the kind,' he said. 'Let the whole situation work itself through, I tell you—it may not be as bad as you think.'

'I don't know what to think.' Her voice was wretched. 'I don't understand anything that's going on.'

'In that case, stay back and wait until things become clearer.' There was a sudden harshness in his tone. 'You're far too fond of leaping to conclusions, usually the wrong ones.'

Alix lifted her chin. 'I suppose you're talking about yourself.'

'You're damned right I am! From the very first, you had me written off as a predator—some kind of literary vulture—and why? Because I let one woman, whose stupidity only equalled her conceit, condemn herself out of her own mouth. You assumed I was going to do a similar job on Bianca, so you leapt to her defence like a female St George against the dragon.'

'And do you blame me?' she defended herself. 'You behaved like an adversary the first time we met—and ever since.'

His mouth twisted slightly. 'We haven't always been adversaries, you and I, Alix—so don't fool yourself. We have a lot going for us—and your body knows it, even if that hostile little mind of yours keeps rejecting the fact.'

'I don't deny that you can make me want you,' she said in a low voice. 'How could I deny it? But I'm not proud of it. You make me despise myself...' Her voice trailed away uncertainly as she saw the anger in his face—anger, and another less easily defined emotion.

'Do I now?' he grated. 'Then add this to your burden of shame, secretary bird.'

His hands were merciless as he pulled her to him, and his mouth savaged hers with ruthless intensity. She couldn't breathe, she could barely think, aware only of a surge of passionate emotion which had her clinging to him helplessly, her fingers digging into the muscular firmness of his shoulders.

The door of her room was just behind them. She wanted to be alone with him in that room, the door closed against the world. The longing consumed her like a fire. It was impossible, she thought dazedly, for her to feel like this and him not be aware of it. The total surrender of her response, the movements of her body against his all evinced the agony of desire which tore her with sharp talons.

At last he put her away from him, detaching her clinging arms from round his neck as he might remove a burr from his jacket. Under his tan, he was very pale.

'I think we'll leave the demonstration there,' he said huskily. 'If it's any consolation to you, Alix, I also despise myself.'

He turned and walked away down the passage, leaving her staring after him, one hand pressed convulsively to her bruised mouth.

After a while, the days began to take on a kind of pattern, Alix discovered. The scene with Liam had left her shattered, and she was glad to have the excuse of work to keep in her room for the rest of the day. And after that it was easy enough to spend her mornings by the pool, usually with Paola, before going to Bianca's suite, timing her arrival to ensure that she never again en-

countered Liam there alone. She would dine downstairs
with everyone else, then go up to her room to transcribe
the day's notes, on the portable typewriter which travelled everywhere with her. Then she would fall into bed
and try to sleep, only to find hours later that she was
still lying, staring at the ceiling, a terrible aching empti-
ness inside her.

The afternoons were torture for her. The rapport between Liam and Bianca seemed total, indicating a deeper
and different intimacy during the hours when they were
not working on the book. Alix tried not to notice, tried
to concentrate on the notes she was taking, and thought
she was succeeding, until the long hours of the night
made her know better.

Liam was there in her mind, behind her eyelids, like a
fixed image, and she had total recall of every gesture,
every movement of his lean body, every nuance as he
spoke. The events of each afternoon paraded themselves
like a constant nightmare.

And the worst part of it was that she was the outsider.
He rose when she entered the suite and seated herself at
the desk, and apart from the odd brusque enquiry if she
was able to keep up, ignored her completely thereafter.

But what else did she expect? she asked herself with a
kind of desperation.

She had thought again about her idea of asking Carlo
to find her another job. He was ebullient, charming and
talented, but he could not be trusted. She didn't want
his help.

Besides, she felt she couldn't just walk out and leave
Bianca in the lurch when at any moment a bombshell
was going to explode in her life. When she returned to
London, she thought, she would apply to one of the
agencies that specialised in temporary work while she
decided what path she wanted her life to take.

Whatever decision she came to, it could only be
second-best, she acknowledged bitterly, even though she
knew there was no future for her with Liam.

But she wasn't the only unhappy occupant of the villa. Leon seized every opportunity to borrow one of Carlo's cars and get away on supposed sightseeing trips, although he admitted to Alix that he rarely went farther than the village where he discovered the parish priest was a keen chess player.

'He beats me every time,' he said ruefully, 'because I can't keep my mind on the game. Bianca asks me every day when the contract for the film is going to be ready for her to sign, and I keep stalling, saying there are still a few details to be finalised, but she won't accept that for ever. I sensed yesterday when I talked to her that she was getting impatient.' He groaned. 'She keeps the damned script on the table beside her bed.'

'Why don't you tell her what's going on—break the conspiracy of silence?' Alix asked.

'Because I'm a coward,' he said frankly. 'Veronese insists that he'll tell her in his own good time, and he's welcome.' He sighed heavily. 'I've been doing my best, of course. I've told her that the script doesn't impress me on a second reading, that the part's badly written, that she oughtn't to rush into anything. She's started to eye me as if I was mad.'

Alix hesitated. 'You remember you told me that Lester was involved somehow. I—I was talking to Liam Brant, and he more or less confirmed it. What's more, Lester's supposed to be arriving here himself any day now.'

Leon groaned. 'My God, that's all we need! Well, he has guts if he's prepared to face Bianca after what he's done to her, I'll say that for him.' He gave her a wan smile and departed, presumably in search of another escape route, but not this time through a bottle, Alix found herself hoping. She didn't want Leon's wife to find she had an alcoholic on her hands when he returned to England.

When the storm finally burst over them, it was out of a

clear blue sky. She had sensed when she arrived at
Bianca's suite that afternoon that the star was restive,
and on edge. Monty came in just as Liam began the
interview and Bianca snapped at her in a way that made
the older woman's mouth tighten grimly as she made
her way to the door.

Alix made herself as inconspicuous as possible. There
could be any number of explanations for Bianca's
sudden ill-temper, she thought. But the uncertainty over
the contract had to come top of the list, not to mention
Leon's hints which might be beginning to bear fruit.

'Shall we get on before there are any more interrup-
tions, and if Alix can be persuaded to come out of her
dream world.' Bianca shot her an acid look. 'I'm sorry,
Liam. What were you saying?'

'I said today we'd start to fill in some of the early
details.'

Bianca pulled a face. 'Darling, people don't want to
read that sort of dreary rubbish. It's all too David
Copperfield.'

'You'd be surprised what people want to know about
their idols.' The charm of his smile softened the usually
cynical lines of his mouth. 'What you've told me so far
is fascinating, but there are gaps, as I'm sure you're
aware.'

There was a pause, then Bianca said petulantly, 'Don't
be a brute, Liam. I'd really much rather talk about
something else. My first film, for instance. I was thinking about that last night, and really the way it happened
was quite amazing . . .'

He said pleasantly, 'Some other time, Bianca. We've
yet to reach that point.' Their glances met and clashed,
and Bianca threw herself back on her cushions looking
sulky.

She said ungraciously, 'As you wish, then. But don't
expect a glowing account of my childhood. I can barely
remember a thing that happened.'

'I'm sure you can remember enough.' He leaned forward and touched a button on the tape-recorder. 'Your parents, for instance—who were they? Are they still alive—do you see them? What other family do you have—sisters—brothers?'

There was a long silence, then Bianca said slowly and reluctantly, 'My father was a civil servant. I believe my mother worked in the same department as a typist, and that's how they met. She didn't work after they were married, of course. I don't think women did then.'

'And she had children to look after,' Liam suggested.

'Yes.' Another silence. 'There were two of us, my sister and myself.'

'Your sister was older than you?'

'Of course,' said Bianca with something of a snap.

'Was there a great gap in your ages? Were you close as children?'

'She was five years older, and no, we were not.'

'Do you ever see her now?'

'As seldom as possible.' The snap was even more evident. 'We have even less in common as adults. Margaret is a suburban housewife without a thought in her head beyond the needs of her family.' She added brusquely, 'I'm sorry, Alix, but I didn't instigate this conversation.'

'Alix, of course, being the daughter of this suburban Margaret, rather than your cousin.'

She said impatiently, 'Yes, if you must know. Does it matter? It didn't suit me to have a grown-up niece. Why the inquisition over a piece of harmless vanity?'

Liam lifted a hand half-deprecatingly. 'Yet you haven't always avoided your sister. There was a time when you spent quite a long period in her company. In fact you took her abroad with you—to Spain, wasn't it?'

Bianca sat up abruptly, letting one of the cushions which supported her fall to the floor. 'She'd been ill. She needed a break. And I'd been overworking. There'd been difficulties over the film I was making around then.'

'*Starlight Madonna*, wasn't it,' Liam prompted casually. 'With Stuart Lisle? I'm not surprised you had problems. He was in the process of drinking himself to death at the time.'

There was another silence, then Bianca said thickly, 'Is there anything—is there—any—damned—thing that you don't already know?'

'Not a great deal,' said Liam. 'As I mentioned, I'm hoping that you'll fill in the missing details.'

'You can hope!' Bianca snapped. 'Switch that bloody machine off. I refuse to answer any more questions.'

Alix stared at her in amazement. She had gone very pale, and the carefully applied blusher stood out vividly along her cheekbones. She was staring at Liam as if she hated him.

'I won't answer another question. Not today, not ever. I've seen through your little game!'

'Its name,' Liam said calmly, 'is reality. Something you may have lost touch with over the years.'

Bianca stared at him, her eyes glittering, her breasts rising and falling. 'Get out, Alix.'

Helplessly Alix rose to her feet.

'What's the matter?' Liam gibed. 'What are you afraid she might hear?'

'Didn't you hear me? I said get out!' Bianca turned on her like a virago.

Alix still hesitated. 'These notes . . .'

'Destroy them,' Bianca ordered. 'Tear them up. Not just these—but all you've done. I don't want to hear another word about them!'

Alix closed the door of the suite behind her and drew a deep breath. What was there between her mother and her aunt, she wondered, that could still evoke such bitterness so many years afterwards?

When she reached her room, she took out the file of transcribed notes and stared at it. She was reluctant to destroy them, because Bianca's viewpoint about the book had already veered several times. The scene she had just witnessed might be just a temporary tantrum, brought on by other frustrations, and tomorrow Bianca might be all smiles.

Liam would get round her, Alix thought with a sigh. He'd done it before.

She took off the blouse and skirt she was wearing, and put on her cotton robe before lying down on her bed. Her head was aching slightly, and the pillow felt cool. Gratefully she closed her eyes. Her restless nights had caught up with her with a vengeance, and it would be easy, so easy just to drift away, and let all her problems and confusions drift with her.

The next thing she was aware of was a hand shaking her shoulder violently. She came awake with a start and sat up to see Monty leaning over her looking distraught.

'What is it?' she asked, pushing her hair back from her face.

'All hell's broken loose, that's all,' Monty retorted. 'She's been working herself into one of her rages since early this morning. I tried to persuade her to leave the villa for a while—go for a drive with Leon, maybe—anything, but she bit my head off. Then she had a row with that Brant fellow over something, and then nothing would do but Signor Veronese must come to the suite to talk to her about the film. She said she was sick and tired of all this pussyfooting around, and where was her contract.'

'Go on,' Alix said tensely.

Monty closed her eyes for a moment. 'He was very civil. He said he would be happy for her to sign a contract to play in the film when a final decision was reached on which part she would play.'

'Oh God,' Alix said hoarsely.

'For a moment,' Monty went on, 'I don't think she understood what he was saying. And then she started to stiffen. She said, "I'm going to play Francesca, of course. It might have been written for me." And he didn't say a word, just stood there watching her. After a minute she said, "I am going to play it. Tell me so, damn you!" And he gave a little bow and said "*Cara*, I regret that it is impossible!"' Monty shuddered. 'I thought she was going to have a heart attack. And then she flew at him. That Brant man grabbed hold of her, and held her off, and then Leon came in not before time, and they made her sit down. She was crying and swearing, calling them all the most terrible names. At the end Signor Veronese slapped her face, and she quietened down. Now she wants to see you.'

'I'll come at once.' Alix swung her legs off the bed, tightening the sash of her robe.

Bianca was lying face downwards on the chaise-longue. As Alix knelt down beside her, putting a tentative hand on her arm, she lifted a ravaged face and stared at her. Her eyes were red and swollen, and there were faint marks on her cheek where she had been slapped. Her usually immaculate hair was dishevelled and coming free from its elaborate chignon.

She said like a child might do, 'They're not going to let me play Francesca. He's going to give it to that bitch, his mistress. I was afraid when I saw her, but I told myself she was just around to keep him amused. But I was wrong. She's going to be Francesca—and do you know what they've offered me. The part of the mother.' Her voice began to rise hysterically again. 'Do you hear me? The mother!'

Alix tried to sound soothing. 'Darling, it isn't the end of the world . . .'

'It's the end of my world,' Bianca whispered. Her hand closed round Alix's, gripping it so tightly that Alix winced. 'I will never—ever—play the part of anyone's mother. Never, do you hear me. I won't! I can't!'

'But why is it so impossible?' Alix asked gently. 'You love the script, you know you do. Can you really bear to say goodbye to it altogether?'

For a moment Bianca stared at her, her feverish gaze

narrowing, then she flung Alix's hand away from her.

'You sound like Leon,' she said accusingly. 'I've sacked him. He's packing his bags at this very moment. Thanks to his bungling I've been subjected to the most horrifying humiliation of my career.'

'But no one intended that,' Alix said, hoping desperately that it was true.

Bianca went on staring at her, then slowly she levered herself into a sitting position, and swung her legs to the ground. And all the time her eyes never left Alix's face, eyes that were suddenly as cold and hard as marble.

Her lips stretched in a mirthless smile. 'Your opinion fascinates me, darling. Is that a wild guess, or, like Leon, did you have advance information?'

Alix realised that she had blundered badly. She said quickly, 'Bianca, please listen to me. It isn't as you think . . .'

'Then how is it?' Bianca asked softly and dangerously. 'It seems like deceit and treachery and lies from people who were close to me, people I thought I could trust.' Her voice was rising. 'You knew, didn't you, Alix? You knew?'

Alix bent her head unhappily. She didn't have to speak.

'Snake!' Bianca accused on a sob. 'You—my own flesh and blood. You little bitch!' Her hand flew out, striking Alix full across the face. Caught off balance, she half fell sideways.

'Bitch!' Bianca shrieked again.

Half dazed by the blow, Alix heard Monty mutter, 'Oh, my God,' and was aware of strong arms lifting her from the floor.

'Get her out of here,' Bianca ordered. 'She's fired! I never want to see her again. Let her go back to London with that other treacherous swine. Get your things from my house and go back where you came from—where I should have left you.'

Alix heard the words as if they were coming from a

distance—as if they had no actual relation to herself. She had been going to give Bianca her notice, she thought, but now it wasn't necessary, because she was leaving anyway. So she didn't have to worry any more, and that was funny, so funny.

She began to laugh, and checked abruptly, as someone shook her sharply.

'That's enough,' ordered Liam. 'One raging hysteric is enough to cope with.'

She was in his arms and he was carrying her. She pushed at his chest.

'Put me down! I can walk.'

'Don't be a fool,' he said crushingly. 'I doubt if you could even crawl.'

He shouldered his way into her room, and put her down on the bed.

'I'll send Graziella to you,' he said curtly, turning away.

Alix said, her voice shaking, 'Liam—don't leave me. Please don't go.'

She needed the warmth and strength of his arms around her, because she was trembling like a leaf, feeling lost and afraid. She had seen Bianca in tempers many times before, but never—never looking as if she hated her. She shuddered, lifting a hand to her throbbing face.

'The sooner you pack and get away from here, the better,' he told her. 'I'll get Carlo to ring the airport and try and get us on the next flight.'

'You—you're coming too?' she asked.

He shrugged. 'There's nothing I can do here. And Marchant is on his way. Let him make her face reality. He should be able to do it, if anyone can.' He paused, then said roughly, 'Don't look so stricken, Alix. You may find it hard to believe, but there's every chance that everything's going to be all right. Now I'll find Graziella, and she can help you pack.'

When he had gone, Alix turned over, burying her face in the pillow. There had been no warmth in his tone, no tenderness, although she supposed she had been a fool to hope for them. He wasn't leaving out of concern for her, but because it was clear that all work on the book had ground to an abrupt halt.

Even while he had been speaking to her, his eyes had been remote, as if his thoughts were elsewhere. And of course Lester Marchant's imminent arrival would have influenced his decision to leave, she thought, feeling a little sob rise in her throat. Lester might no longer be Bianca's legal husband, but that didn't mean he would welcome finding her lover in residence at the villa when he arrived.

She sighed wearily. No matter how bitter her conclusions, it made no difference. She loved Liam, she was starving for him, and if these few crumbs of comfort from his company as far as London were all that there were for her, then she would savour every last one.

Because only too soon even they would be denied to her.

CHAPTER EIGHT

It was nearly dawn when the taxi drew up outside the house. It had been an uneventful flight. Leon had slept most of the way, his attitude one of gloomy resignation. He had not the slightest confidence in Lester Marchant's ability to resolve the crisis, which he considered was all of his own making anyway. In fact he confided to Alix in an undertone that Bianca would probably have an apoplexy when she saw him.

Alix could not sleep. She sat rigidly in her seat beside Liam, staring at an airline magazine without taking in one word of it. When the stewardess came round with drinks she asked for fruit juice, but Liam said curtly, 'She'll have a brandy,' and ordered himself a straight whisky.

Full circle, she thought wryly. On the outward flight she had ordered brandy for Monty. Such a short time ago, and yet in that brief space her whole life had changed.

Monty had taken a surprisingly emotional leave of her. 'I never agreed with her employing you—I knew it would end in disaster,' she had said huskily. 'But I never thought it would be like this.'

Alix had been touched too by a warm hug from Paola. 'I shall miss our mornings by the pool,' she said. 'But we'll meet again, Alix, you'll see.'

Carlo's farewell was more practical, making sure she had sufficient cash to tide her over, and somewhere to stay once she had collected her belongings from the London house.

'Poor little one,' he said. 'It was never intended that you become a victim of all this, and that is my only regret.'

'Your only regret?' Alix gave him a steady look, but he was unabashed, shrugging and giving her a charming smile.

'You do not approve, of course, but it was necessary. No star shines for ever—the days when this was possible are gone. The lovely virago upstairs must face this or go to the wall as others have done. I still hope that she can be induced to come to terms with reality, and that this may not be the end for her, but yet another beginning. One must be cruel to be kind, is that not what they say?'

In spite of that, Alix could not help thinking that the methods which had been used had involved considerable cruelty without a great deal of kindness.

She was trying hard to blank the scene with Bianca out in her mind. She had often imagined that she would probably depart after some unholy uproar, but the actuality had been worse than anything she could ever have dreamed of. She had not thought it possible that she could feel so hurt and—abandoned. And yet she should have realised that she could expect nothing better from Bianca, so her disappointment and unhappiness were quite out of proportion to her sense of realism.

And she would have to go home and admit to her family that her glamorous job hadn't worked out after all. Her parents would probably be relieved, and try not to show it, and Debbie—well, Debbie would be triumphant.

Alix bit her lip. She had managed to put her family problems to the back of her mind while she was in Italy, but now they had to be faced head-on once more, and she dreaded the prospect.

She had expected Liam to drop her at the house and take the taxi on to his own flat, and she was therefore surprised when he paid off the driver, and carried his suitcase as well as hers up the steps.

'What's the matter?' His voice was impatient. 'Can't you find your key? I presume you have one.'

'Yes—of course,' Alix stammered, searching through her bag, and producing it.

'Give it to me.' He held his hand out, but she hesitated. 'Or would you rather ring the bell, and have us admitted in due form, under the circumstances?'

'There isn't anyone to admit us,' she told him. 'The Harrises are taking a holiday. They won't be back until next week.'

'Then I'll definitely have the key,' he said grimly. 'Wait here while I check that everything's all right.'

Shivering a little in the chill early morning breeze, Alix stood on the step, watching as the lights came on and went off on all three floors, marking his progress through the house. As he came down the stairs, she walked into the hall and closed the door beside her.

'Thank you,' she said stiltedly.

The dark brows drew together in a frown. 'You look half dead,' he remarked coolly. 'Go and sit down in there'—he nodded towards the drawing room—'and I'll bring you some coffee. Yes, I do know where the kitchen is, and where everything's kept,' he added sardonically, forestalling her objection.

'Yes, I suppose you do,' she muttered, remembering the numerous evening *tête-à-têtes* he had enjoyed in this house, which she had so desperately tried to ignore. 'But you really don't have to bother.'

'It isn't any bother. I could do with some coffee myself.'

Alix wandered into the drawing room, and stood looking round her. The air smelt stale, and there was a definite chill in the air. It would soon be time for the central heating to be switched on again, but as she no longer officially lived there, Alix could not take so much on herself, so she compromised by switching on a couple of bars of the big electric fire which formed the focal point of the rather grandiose marble fireplace at one end of the room.'

She sank down on the huge fur rug which fronted the

hearth and stretched out her hands as the bars began to glow, but no amount of surface heat was going to dispel the coldness she felt inside.

Liam came in carrying a tray. 'No fresh milk, of course, so it has to be this powdered stuff,' he said. 'But at least it will be hot.'

The coffee was in two pottery mugs. Alix surmised that they must belong to the Harrises, because she was quite sure Bianca would never have bought anything quite so basic and functional for her own use. She clasped her hands gratefully round the warmth emanating from the earthenware.

Liam had flung himself down on one of the sofas. He had discarded the fine wool tweed jacket he had worn on the flight, and loosened his tie. He looked very much at home, Alix thought stonily.

She said, 'I'd better go up and start packing. I'll take my coffee with me. If you could be sure to slam the front door behind you when you leave . . .'

'Naturally.' He gave her an unsmiling glance. 'But I wouldn't be in too much hurry to pack. You could do with some sleep first.'

'I think Bianca intended that I should collect my things and be on my way as soon as possible.' She tried to smile and failed.

'Bianca's not here,' he said tersely. 'And I'm telling you that you'll make a far more efficient job of your packing when you're rested. Where do you plan to go when you leave here?'

'Home, I suppose,' she said, smothering a sigh, as she remembered that Debbie had totally appropriated the room they had once shared long ago, and that Margaret had adapted the other bedroom for her sewing. There was a bed in there somewhere, under the boxes of paper patterns, the dressmaker's dummy, and the current half-finished garment, but she would do far better to find herself a hotel room for a few nights. After all, she could well afford it, but she didn't want to give Liam the impression that she was an orphan of the storm. The last thing she wanted was his pity, she thought passionately.

'The idea doesn't seem to set you afire with expectation.' His lips twisted. 'Where is home?'

'A semi-detached in the suburbs,' she said coolly. She glanced around her, smiling slightly. 'I've become spoiled, you see.'

'I wouldn't have described it in quite those terms,' Liam said drily. 'It isn't just the surroundings that you'll miss, though, or am I wrong?'

She bent her head. 'No,' she said quietly.

There was a pause, then he said roughly, 'Bianca doesn't deserve you, Alix.'

'Well, she doesn't have me any more,' she returned with bravado, then gulped suddenly as an involuntary sob rose in her throat. She rose hurriedly, avoiding the searching look which Liam sent her. 'You're right—I am very tired, and I don't suppose Bianca would grudge me a few more hours under her roof.'

'As long as she never knows anything about it, I imagine not,' he said cynically. 'Off you go, secretary bird. How do you ultimately propose to get to your suburban semi-detached?'

'I'll telephone my father and ask him to collect me,' she said hastily. 'Please don't worry about me,' she added rather stiffly.

'Don't be a fool, Alix,' he advised wearily. 'Now go to bed, before I lose my temper and forget all my good resolutions regarding you.'

And she didn't even want to begin to consider the implications in that, Alix thought wildly. Coffee in hand, she hesitated rather uncertainly. 'You won't forget what I said about the door?'

'No, I won't forget,' he said, raising his eyebrows impatiently. 'Your instructions weren't exactly complicated.'

'No.' She lingered still, because it had occurred to her that she might never see him again. Oh, there'd be television interviews, and photos on the jackets of books, but never again like this. Alone with him, when only a few steps would take her to him—into his arms . . .

It took all the self-control she could dredge up for her to turn away.

'Goodnight, Alix.' His voice followed her. 'Although that's hardly appropriate. Good morning, perhaps?'

'Or goodbye,' her lips framed silently.

Upstairs, she moved like an automaton, turning on the immersion heater, so that later there would be warm water for a shower at least, fetching bedding for her stripped bed from the neat piles in the linen cupboard, then shedding her clothes and slipping in between the sheets, pulling the soft weight of the duvet closely around her for comfort.

In spite of her unhappiness, she was on the edge of sleep when she heard the front door slam, and the echo of that and her silent goodbye accompanied her into her first troubled doze.

Gradually as her tired body and mind relaxed, deeper sleep came, but accompanied by vague troubled dreams. Dreams which made her twist and turn, seeking a cool place on the pillows.

She was back in the Italian garden, walking down the paths which led to the sundial, but as she walked, the small clipped hedges grew rapidly, transforming the garden into a maze where she was hopelessly trapped. And yet she knew if she could reach the sundial in the centre, she would be safe.

She began to run, feeling tears wet on her face, while the hedges towered over her, twigs and leaves catching at her clothes as she brushed past them. She cried out, and in the distance, in the middle of the maze she heard Liam call her name. With a little moan, she ran forward again, her hands reaching out eagerly, then tripped and fell—and felt Liam's hands on her shoulders, lifting her, turning her towards him.

His voice said, 'Easy, darling. You're just having a bad dream, that's all. Everything's all right.'

She opened her eyes, and the nightmare garden withered and died. She was in her own room, in bed, and the sun she had imagined blazing down at her was her bedside lamp.

Liam was bending over her, his dark face harsh with concern.

She asked huskily, 'What time is it?'

'Almost eight o'clock. You've nearly slept the clock round.'

It was incredible. It seemed to Alix that she had only just closed her eyes. And something else was wrong too.

She said slowly, 'Why are you here? I heard you leave—I know I did.'

He smiled. 'You heard me go out for some milk and bread and a paper. Did you really imagine I was going to vanish, leaving you on your own?'

She said carefully, 'I shall be all right. You really don't have to bother about me.'

'Alix, you little fool!' His voice was an exasperated groan, and he pulled her towards him, the sheltering quilt falling away from her shoulders as his mouth crushed hers possessively. For a moment she resisted, her fingers spreading against the warm wall of his chest, but touching him, feeling the quickened thud of his heart under her palms was a seduction in itself, and helplessly she found herself surrendering to a clamour in her blood which drowned the last whisper of common sense.

He sank down beside her on the bed, the weight of his body holding her in sensuous captivity. She was returning his kisses with her whole heart, her mouth hectic and feverish beneath his, no longer caring that every kiss, every caress was proclaiming her secret.

'This to remember,' she thought somewhere on the edge of her mind. 'At least I'll have this to remember.'

Liam was kissing her throat, his mouth warm and sure as it moved over her flesh, and down to the curve of her shoulders, his fingers sliding the straps of her nightdress down to bare her skin for his further exploration. Her body arched up towards him in blind submission, the lacy bodice of her nightgown falling away from the small high breasts.

He paused, looking down at her, breathing sharply and unevenly, his dark gaze seeming to devour the treasures his passionate demand had uncovered for him. Then a long shuddering sigh went through him, and the dark head bent so that his mouth could take possession of her.

Her head fell back, and she heard a little moan deep in her throat as her ungiven body savoured for the first time the piercing sweetness of his caresses. Nothing had prepared her for the dark vein of sensuality in her own nature, or the way its heat was pervading her entire body, urging her to kiss as she was kissed, touch as she was touched, totally satisfying the hunger that was consuming her. Liam's lips were patterning on her skin, drawing tiny spirals of excitement on the warm flesh while his tongue gently stroked the rosy nipples into peaks of aching delight.

His hands slid down her body, taking her nightgown with them, his fingers warm and sensuous as he stripped her. He lifted himself away from her, and looked down at her as if he couldn't credit the surrender implied in her nakedness.

'God, Alix, I want you,' he muttered unsteadily. 'You're so lovely. I've dreamed of this moment—of seeing you, kissing you, knowing every inch of you.'

No word of love, she registered with a pang. She had to accept that was a commitment he neither wished to make nor required from her.

Her voice was ragged as she said, 'I want you, Liam. But I'm not—I haven't—I don't know how to please you,' she ended on a little rush of words.

His mouth twisted wryly, tenderly. He said, 'Obey your instincts, my sweet. I'll try and make it easy for you.' His hands smoothed a strand of damp hair back from her brow. 'All you need give is yourself, Alix. We have to learn to please each other, and this is only the beginning.'

He kissed her mouth, and his hands touched her with lingering gentleness, cupping her breasts, then sliding downwards over the taut planes of her stomach to her hips, and the silky firmness of her thighs.

She began to kiss him in turn, her mouth burning against his throat while her shaking fingers tugged open the buttons of his shirt. Her hands slid inside his shirt, revelling in the strength of bone and muscle, the warmth of his skin, as if she was absorbing the essence of him through her own pores.

Liam pushed himself into a kneeling position and shrugged off his shirt, tossing it to the floor beside the bed. His hands went to his belt, and he said huskily, 'Help me, darling.'

Alix was trembling as she obeyed. When she had finished, he took her in his arms, and held her against him until the shaking stopped, as if there was all the time in the world, as if the touch of their bodies in this close embrace was enough.

When he kissed her, his mouth seemed to convey a new urgency, and her own senses flamed in response, eagerly, longingly. She began to match his caresses, her hands moving without inhibition over his body, making him groan with pleasure.

'Don't, Alix,' he ordered thickly. 'I want to be gentle, but you're making it impossible . . .'

She didn't need his gentleness. She was on fire for him, and whatever pain he might inflict would be only a small price to pay for the satisfaction of this agony of desire he had aroused in her. She kissed his mouth fiercely, her small teeth grazing his lower lip.

Her fingers biting into his shoulders, her slender legs entwined with his, she fell back with him on to the tumbled pillows and the conflagration consumed them both.

*

A long time later, she said dreamily, 'I'm hungry.'

Liam lifted his head from its pillow on her breast, and looked at her. 'For food or for me?'

'Hm,' she pretended to consider. 'For food—first,' she added in laughing haste as his mock scowl threatened reprisals. 'Did you get anything else besides milk and bread?'

'Some eggs, cheese and bacon.' He kissed the tip of her nose.

'What efficiency!' she marvelled. 'You must have known you'd be staying for breakfast.'

He shook his head, his eyes caressing her. 'I only knew I was staying. And it's supper, actually.'

'So it is,' she said, her heart beginning to thud again as her eyes met his, and shared the unspoken message— that the whole night lay ahead of them.

She slipped out of bed and picked up her discarded nightgown, pulling it on over her head. Liam stayed where he was, lying relaxedly, his hands linked behind his head, watching her every move.

He said softly, 'I hope you don't expect me to dress for dinner.'

Alix shrugged. 'I wouldn't dream of dictating about such a thing,' she countered lightly, reaching for her robe. 'I have to put something on—just in case we get any unexpected visitors.'

'We'd better not,' Liam said forcefully. He threw back the quilt, and got out of bed. He came over to her, drawing her into his arms. He said, 'Alix—if I said I regretted anything that's happened here, it would be a lie, and we both know it. But I didn't intend this to happen—at least not now, not like this.'

She laid a finger across his lips. 'Don't say any more, Liam. Don't spoil it.' She tried to smile.

'Spoil it?' He was frowning. 'What the hell are you talking about? I only wanted to say . . .' He broke off abruptly, as the sound of the telephone suddenly shrilled through the quiet house. 'My God!' he muttered disgustedly. 'You wished this on us. Don't answer it.'

'Of course I must,' she said. 'It—it might be Italy.' It might be Bianca, she thought, ringing to make sure that the house was empty. Or ringing to find out where Liam was.

'Then tell whoever it is that it's a wrong number,' he said. He gave her a swift hard kiss.

Alix went into the office, and lifted the receiver. She began, 'Miss Layton's . . .' but before she could get any further, Gemma's voice broke in. 'Oh, Alix is that you? I didn't know what to do—where to telephone. I thought there might be someone there who could give me your Italian number.'

'Gemma? What is it?' Alix knew a sharp pang of foreboding.

'It's your mother. I only found out a little while ago. Alix, she's in hospital. She's had to have a major operation—a mastectomy. I—I couldn't believe it. I knew they hadn't told you.'

Alix said hoarsely, 'Oh God—it can't be true! Is she all right?'

'I think so. I asked your father, and he said she was making an excellent recovery. He seemed embarrassed at me asking, and Debbie was furious. She as good as told me it was none of my business.'

'Which hospital is she in? The General?' Alix questioned tautly.

'Yes, but she's leaving there, and going into a private nursing home to convalesce. Debbie wouldn't tell me which one.'

Alix sighed. 'Gemma, I can't thank you enough. I'll go to the house and find out exactly what's going on.'

'That's probably best,' said Gemma. 'Alix, she may be your sister, but Debbie wants a damned good hiding. Keep in touch, love.'

Alix replaced her receiver, and began to shake.

From behind her, Liam demanded, 'Who's in hospital? What the hell's going on?'

She thought, 'He thinks it's Bianca—that there's something the matter with Bianca.'

She said, 'It's my mother. She's very ill. She's had to have an operation, and they didn't tell me. They don't want me to know.' Her voice broke. 'My father—my sister—they didn't tell me. They knew where I was going. They could have got a message to me somehow—through Leon's office—somehow.'

He said roughly, 'Alix, don't! At least you know now. What do you want to do?'

'I must go to her,' she said on a little sob. 'I must!'

'Then you shall.' His voice sounded soothing, and the hand which stroked her hair back from her face was gentle too. 'We'll get dressed, and then I'll go and fetch my car while you make that meal we were going to have.'

She said, 'I haven't got time to wait for all that. I'll get a taxi. I have to leave now—at once!'

Liam's hands gripped her arms. He said as if repeating something to a child, 'We'll go together—after we've eaten. I'll drive you there. You shouldn't face this alone.'

'Face what?' she echoed wildly. 'The fact that my sister seems to hate me enough to keep my mother's illness from me? I've already faced that. Or do you know something that I didn't—about the operation, perhaps?' She shook his hands from her and stepped back. 'You can tell me, Liam. Was the operation—too late?'

He said rather wearily, 'I'm sorry if I've misled you, Alix. I know nothing at all about your mother's condition, its treatment or her post-operative condition. I just don't think you're in any fit state to be alone. Please stop arguing—it only wastes time—and do as I say.'

He turned and left her standing staring at the silent telephone. When she returned to the bedroom, he was already dressed and on his way downstairs.

'I'm going to fetch the car now,' he flung over his

shoulder. 'Have food ready for us both by the time I come back.'

Alix showered and dressed, and went downstairs. She tried to telephone her parents' house, but the line was engaged. Then she tried a local mini-cab firm, only to be told there was no car free. She replaced the receiver with a little bitter sigh, then went into the kitchen. He had bought gammon steaks, she discovered, and she put these to grill, while she percolated coffee, and sliced bread for the toaster. By the time he returned, the steaks were ready, and the eggs were just beginning to scramble in the pan.

'Good girl,' he said, sitting down at the table, and she felt sudden tears, thick and sharp in her throat at the casual approbation in his voice. She wasn't hungry, but she made herself eat, and tried not to think how different this meal could have been. When they had finished, she rinsed the dishes and put them in the dishwasher.

He drove well, she discovered, as the car made its way out of the city. There were too many lights about—traffic signals, neon signs, the headlights of other cars, and she leaned back in her seat, closing her eyes.

Liam's voice jolted her back. 'I think I know the way to the hospital, but if we're going to the house you'll have to guide me.'

'We'd better go to the house. They may have moved her from the hospital by now,' she said. She noticed that neither of them had said 'home'. 'It's right at the next traffic lights, and then left almost immediately.'

He nodded, and the car moved forward smoothly as the lights changed.

She could see light showing through a chink in the front room curtains when she got to the house. She got out of the car and walked up the path. She had her own key. It was somewhere in the bottom of her bag, but instead she rang the bell.

After a pause the front door opened and Philip

Coulter peered out at her, blinking almost incredulously.

'Alix? Good God, is that you?'

'Yes, Dad,' she said steadily. 'Please may I come in?'

Her father glanced almost uncertainly back over his shoulder. 'Why, yes, dear. Of course.'

'Or do you have to ask Debbie's permission?' Alix enquired bitterly as they stepped into the hall.

Philip Coulter winced. 'Things haven't been easy for Debbie. Try and understand,' he began.

'And it didn't occur to either of you that if I'd been here I could have helped?' Alix shook her head. 'Dad, you look as if you haven't slept for a week. Why didn't you let me know what had happened? When did it begin?'

Debbie said, 'You weren't told because I didn't want you to be.' She stood in the doorway of the living room. Paul stood behind her looking embarrassed.

'The choice shouldn't have been yours,' Alix rounded on her. 'It was my right to know . . .'

'You have no rights in this house,' Debbie said inimically.

'Debbie,' her father appealed weakly. 'This isn't the time or the place . . .'

'Why not?' she flared. 'She might as well know sooner rather than later.'

'Know what?' Alix felt near breaking point. She felt Liam's fingers close round her elbow, supporting her. 'For God's sake, Debbie, what have I done, to be treated like an outsider?'

'You're treated like one, because you are one.' Debbie made no attempt to control the spite in her tone. 'I had to find my birth certificate some time ago so that we could apply for the marriage licence, as it happens, and yours was there too, in a separate envelope and sealed up. It just said "Alix" on it, and I wondered why, so I opened it.'

'Debbie!' her father appealed, his face disturbed.

'Don't say any more. Let your mother and me speak to Alix—later, when all this is over.'

'You tell her?' Debbie sneered. 'Just like you've told her all these years, I suppose. You never had any intention of telling her the truth. You and Mum were quite happy to go on letting her think she was your child, when really she was that slut's bastard—and she couldn't even be bothered to bring her up!' Her voice rose almost hysterically.

Alix could feel all the blood draining out of her face. It was a curious sensation, and she wondered quite objectively if she was going to faint.

She said, 'I don't understand—Debbie, what are you saying?'

'Oh, do let me explain, as Mum explained to me.' Debbie's tone was savage. 'She'd been having an affair, your beautiful mother, with a drunken actor in some film she was in, and she was pregnant. These days it wouldn't matter a damn, but it mattered then. It would have affected her career, the type of casting she got. Bianca Layton was aiming for the top, and a fatherless child was going to be a drag all the way. So she persuaded her only sister who'd been wanting a baby, but hadn't had any luck yet——' she almost spat the words '—to go abroad with her to stay with her, and eventually to pretend that the baby, when it was born, was hers. And Mum agreed. With the money Bianca gave her, she and Dad moved here, so that their old neighbours wouldn't gossip over this sudden miraculous pregnancy.'

Alix said very quietly, 'No—oh, no.'

'She had you, and she gave you away, but she wouldn't let Mum and Dad adopt you. She was too selfish for that. She just promised that she would stay away, but in the end she didn't even keep her word about that. She was rich and famous, and she came and took you away, just to slap Mum and Dad in the face, and make them see that in spite of everything they'd done for you, you were still her child at heart, with an eye to the main chance just like her!'

Alix's hand swung out and hit Debbie hard across her cheek. She heard the younger girl's squeal of outrage, but ignored it, turning to Philip Coulter.

She said between rigid lips, 'I don't have to ask if this is true. A lot of things make sense to me now.'

'Get out!' Debbie cried. 'Get out now. We don't want you here any more. You're her child. Go back to her—to your loving mother. All these years I've had to share everything with you—had to look up to you because you were the oldest. You cheated me, Alix, you took my birthright, the love that should only have been mine, and I never want to see you again. Paul, get her out of here!'

Paul, clearly wishing he was dead, took a reluctant step forward. Liam interposed himself in front of Alix. He said pleasantly, 'Touch her and I'll make you wish you hadn't.'

He was at least a head taller than Paul, who hesitated, casting an appealing look at Debbie.

'I'm not having this,' Philip Coulter said with sudden energy. 'Debbie, I never thought I would ever feel ashamed that you were my daughter, but I am—bitterly ashamed. Alix, my dear child—we've got to talk.'

Liam said coldly, 'Isn't it a little late for that?'

Philip looked wretched. 'We discussed telling her a hundred times, but it never seemed appropriate, and besides, we'd given our word.'

'How very noble!' Liam's voice bit. 'So, having decided it was all going to be your little secret, what a pity you didn't keep it a little more closely guarded, or did you imagine a sealed envelope would be proof against your—daughter's curiosity?'

Philip shrugged helplessly. 'I think Margaret had forgotten it was there. It never occurred to us that Debbie had any cause to go searching among the family papers. We didn't even realise she knew where they were kept.'

He looked miserably at the floor. 'Anyway, now you have the whole story.'

'Yes,' Liam said softly, 'I have the whole story.'

Alix stared at him, her eyes widening in a kind of horror.

Philip shook his head as if he had been mesmerised, and was slowly coming round. 'I don't think we've been introduced.' He held out his hand. 'Clearly you're a friend of Alix's, and I'm sure she'll have mentioned your name, but . . .'

'I've never mentioned his name,' Alix said. 'And he's no friend of mine. As a matter of fact, he's a writer, and at the moment he's trying to collect enough material for a biography about—about Bianca. I think we've provided him with more than enough.'

She turned, wrenching at the front door, and ran down the path, gulping in fresh air, fighting off the nausea that threatened. Liam caught up with her at the gate, swinging her round to face him, his fingers digging cruelly into her flesh.

'Where do you think you're going?'

'Anywhere—as long as it's away from you,' she said wildly.

His grip tightened, and she gave a little cry of pain. 'Don't be a fool!'

'Oh, I've been a fool—I admit that, but it's over now. I thought you were being kind, bringing me here, but it wasn't anything to do with kindness. You knew what was going to happen, didn't you, and that's why you came here. You're a hunter, Liam, and you smelled blood and wanted to be in at the kill.'

'I didn't know what was going to happen here—how could I?' he said roughly. 'But I admit I suspected that you and Bianca enjoyed a closer relationship than she was prepared to admit. That first time I saw you on the stairs—God, you were so like her—the pictures I'd seen of her when she was your age. And then the next time I saw you, you were unrecognisable, like a flame that had been dowsed, in that disguise she made you wear. She was terrified that people would see the resemblance.'

'Poor Bianca,' Alix said tightly. 'She didn't allow for your persistence, did she, Liam? I hope your publishers appreciate just how far you carried your researches, and reward you adequately. Thirty pieces of silver used to be the going rate, I believe.'

He let go of her so suddenly that she staggered and almost fell. His eyes were blazing as he looked at her. 'And what the hell's that supposed to mean?'

The desire to hit back, to salve her own pain by inflicting wounds, was suddenly quenched in Alix. Her shoulders slumped defeatedly. 'It doesn't matter. You've got what you wanted, Liam, and all I hope is that I never have to see you again.'

'Then your hope is destined to remain unfulfilled,' he said between his teeth. 'We're going back to the house now, to get some sleep, because tomorrow we're flying back to Italy.'

'To provide you with some dialogue for the dramatic reunion?' A sob rose in her throat. 'I won't do it.'

'No,' he said. 'To provide you with your real mother, and give you both a chance to care about each other.'

'Care?' she repeated, and gave a little incredulous laugh. 'Oh, she cared. She cared so much, she gave me away to her sister.'

'And then she took you back again. Don't be vindictive, Alix. Just imagine her position. Her career was just taking off, she was in love, and she'd just realised the man she loved was a hopeless alcoholic. If she'd cared as little as you think, she'd have had an abortion. But instead she carried you, and gave birth to you, and then did her best for you by making sure you were brought up in a decent, loving home. Oh, I'm not suggesting her motives were totally altruistic, but what kind of a childhood would you have had if she'd kept you, being dragged round by nannies in Bianca's wake? And she couldn't have known then how quickly the climate of morality was going to change.'

Alix bit her lip. 'I can't wait to read this,' she said. 'There won't be a dry eye in the house. All right, Liam, I'm convinced. Bianca's a saint and I'm the luckiest girl in the world. But I'm not going to Italy or anywhere else with you. I could have warned Bianca about Carlo Veronese and I didn't. When you see her, you can tell her that you could have warned me about this, yet you didn't, so it all cancels out quite neatly. I hope she appreciates the joke.'

'I could have warned you about what? My suspicions? Supposing I'd been wrong.' He shook his head. 'I couldn't risk that. But all the same I had this gut feeling that I ought to stay close to you.'

'Ah, you excelled at that,' she said in bitter mockery. 'How very close you did stay, to be sure. I think I want to be sick.'

His head went back as if she had struck him. 'Say what you want, Alix, but it doesn't change a thing. Only an hour or so ago, you were going crazy in my arms.'

She winced, rejecting the memories he had deliberately evoked.

'Well, I'm sane again now, and I intend to stay that way. You don't have to stand guard over me any longer. Just leave me alone from now on. Go and confront Bianca with what you know. Get some more quotes for the Book of the Year, but didn't expect any help from me.' She gave an unsteady laugh. 'You told me tonight to obey my instincts. Well, I wish to heaven I'd obeyed my earliest one and avoided you like the plague. At least I'd still have my self-respect.'

For a moment Liam looked at her, and she saw a muscle jerk and quiver in his face, then he turned and walked out of the gate. She watched him climb into his car, and heard the engine roar into life. Her hands gripped the garden gate so tightly that her knuckles turned white as she saw the tail-lights disappear down the road.

She thought, 'That's it. Over. All over.'

In the space of a few hours, her entire world had been turned upside down. Now she belonged nowhere, and to no one, and standing in the darkness at the gate of the house she had always thought of as her home, Alix felt alone, afraid and very desolate.

CHAPTER NINE

'Now,' said Gemma for the umpteenth time, 'are you sure you'll be all right? There's masses of food in the fridge for supper—that's if I really can't persuade you to go with us.'

Alix smiled at her from the floor cushion she was occupying near the fire. 'You certainly can't. Candlelit suppers are for two, not three.' She raised her eyebrows as David called impatiently from the front door, 'Gemma, are you ever coming?'

'Yes, O master,' Gemma muttered as she hastily shovelled her purse, keys, compact and lipstick from one bag to another, and cast a frantic look round the room as if she was expecting it to collapse in a pile of dust as soon as she turned her back on it.

'Go,' Alix urged, 'or you'll be celebrating a divorce instead of a wedding anniversary!'

'But I feel awful leaving you here by yourself.' Gemma snarled at her reflection in the mirror above the fireplace and tweaked unavailingly at an errant curl. 'Yes, I'm coming,' she shrieked back, as another despairing bellow was heard from the direction of the front door. 'My God, this meal had better be worth all the hassle!'

Alix responded to their last shouted 'goodbyes', then the front door banged, and she was alone.

She grimaced slightly. Alone was a word she had tried to cut out of her vocabulary over the past weeks, and with Gemma and David's help, she had almost succeeded.

After Liam had driven off that night, Philip had come awkwardly down the path and tried to persuade her to go back to the house, but she had refused. She couldn't face Debbie's hostility again so soon.

Instead, she had walked round the corner to Gemma's house, and Gemma had taken one look at her white face and blank tearless eyes and firmly drawn her inside. David, who had been dozing in front of the television, had been dispatched to make coffee, and when Alix had finished hers, she was taken upstairs to the spare bedroom where clean cotton sheets and a hotwater bottle awaited her. Left to herself, she had eventually cried herself into an exhausted sleep. When she had finally presented herself downstairs the following day, Gemma had asked no questions, making it clear that any confidence would have to be volunteered.

But Alix needed to talk, although it hadn't been easy at first. The words came stiffly and jerkily, and she was thankful that she had cried all her tears away the previous night. Gemma had listened without prompting, without comment as Alix stumbled through her faltering recital, her eyes wide and grave as she watched her friend.

When Alix had finished she said, 'And did you never suspect anything—while you were living with Bianca, I mean?'

Alix shook her head. 'In many ways, she did her best to keep me at a distance,' she said. 'Except once—in Italy, when she came to my room to talk to me. There was almost a closeness then.'

'What did she want?' Gemma asked.

Alix smiled mirthlessly, 'To warn me not to get involved with Liam. I should have listened to her.'

Gemma gave her arm a comforting squeeze. 'Don't punish yourself about that, Alix. You're a human girl, not some kind of saint.'

'But I knew what he was,' Alix said miserably. 'I knew from the start that he was ruthless and unscrupulous, and that I couldn't trust him. Only . . .'

'Only when the chips were down, it made not the slightest difference.' Gemma sounded matter-of-fact. 'Love isn't a computer dating service, you know. It doesn't set up matches between equally worthy and upright citizens. It creates a chemistry and waits for the reaction, which can often be quite explosive—as you've discovered. Now, can you look me in the eye and say that you wish it had never happened—because even if you did I don't think I'd believe you, Alix.'

Alix said soberly, 'I don't think I'd believe myself.'

This was what hurt, she thought later. Knowing that in spite of everything that had happened, she still loved Liam, and that although she knew he had only been using her, if he came to her again she would be unable to resist.

Going back to the house to collect her things had been a painful experience, and she was glad that Gemma went with her. The Harrises had returned from their holiday by then, and although they made no comment, Alix could tell they were surprised to hear that she was leaving. They asked if she knew when Miss Layton would be returning, and she had to confess she had no idea.

She had wanted to start hunting for another job right away, and to answer some of the advertisements for girls to share flats, but Gemma wouldn't hear of it.

'Don't rush into anything,' she advised firmly. 'You're not flat broke, so take your time and look around.'

Alix had also been to visit Margaret in the hospital. She didn't go to the house again, but rang Philip Coulter at work and asked him to meet her. At first he had protested, saying that as far as he was concerned the house was still her home, but she had been quietly insistent that while Debbie's resentment and hostility persisted, she would keep away.

'But I very much want to see——' she hesitated. She had been going to say 'Mum', but substituted 'my aunt' instead. It sounded awkward and formal, but it was a curious situation to be in.

Philip sounded relieved. 'She's been hoping for a visit from you,' he said. 'She was very upset by Debbie's behaviour, naturally. I'd rather have kept it from her for a while, until she was completely over the operation, but it was impossible.' He paused. 'Alix dear, just because there was never an official adoption don't imagine we ever regarded you as anything less than ours. Nothing's really changed.'

She heard the affection and the anxiety in his voice, and agreed gently that nothing had changed, although she knew, as he must, that nothing could ever be the same again. Debbie was there like a barrier, and while both Philip and Margaret might deplore her conduct, she was nevertheless their own child, and Alix could not compete with her for their affection.

Margaret was making a good recovery, but she was still quite weak and inclined to be tearful when she saw Alix.

'I never thought it would turn out like this,' she said, holding Alix's hand. 'We'd been married quite a few years, and I'd begun to give up hope of having a baby. Bianca and I had never got on, not even as children, but when she came to see me—and begged me to help her— well, it seemed like a miracle. We went abroad together for a while, and then we came back without telling anyone except Philip and went up to Northumberland, and that's where you were born.' A reminiscent smile touched her lips. 'There was a little cottage hospital there, and the midwife came out of the delivery room and put you in my arms. You were so lovely. I felt so happy that it didn't seem that anything could ever go wrong, although Philip was dubious from the beginning.'

'Then why didn't you adopt me officially?' Alix asked.

Margaret shook her head. 'Bianca wouldn't agree. She wouldn't even discuss it. She said she'd given you to me, so what more did I want? She swore that she'd keep away, that she'd never make any claims on you, but I was always anxious. And then, as so often happens apparently, I found I was expecting Debbie.' She gave a little laugh. 'Two children to love, when I'd thought there wouldn't be any!' She sobered. 'And Bianca—all those marriages, and yet never a sign of another baby. It's sadly ironic.' She sighed. 'I suppose I knew all along that one day she'd come back. That she wouldn't be able to resist seeing you, discovering how you'd turned out. I saw her watching you that day, and I knew that somehow she was going to take you away from me.' She lifted a hand and touched Alix's cheek. 'That's what she's done as well, what I was so afraid of.'

'No,' Alix said quietly. 'She could never do that. All my earliest memories are of you—and—and Dad. How could she possibly expect ever to come first with me?'

Margaret's lips twisted ruefully. 'But she is your mother, Alix. She saw you first, held you first—chose your name . . .' her voice trailed away.

As you did for Debbie, Alix thought. She got up from her chair. 'You're looking tired, darling. I'd better go before Sister scolds me.'

'Sister scolds everyone.' Margaret leaned back against her pillows. 'Look at my lovely flowers—the Mothers' Union sent them. And the plant is from Mrs Henderson next door.'

As Alix reached the door, she suddenly said, 'Don't hate her, darling. Being ill like this has made me see a lot of things more clearly. She wasn't being totally selfish. She didn't want you to grow up with a slur of illegitimacy about you. Even in these permissive days people don't approve of unmarried mothers. It was infinitely worse then, but I don't think Bianca realised until you were born how hard she was going to find it to give you up.'

Alix looked back gravely at the pale woman in the bed. 'I don't hate her,' she said. 'I never have—even in her worst moments. At times I've felt almost protective towards her, so it's ironic that I should now be the cause of all this trouble for her.'

'Because of this book, you mean,' Margaret said vaguely. 'Your father mentioned something about it— that the writer had been at the house that night. It's all most unfortunate. Will he use the information, do you suppose?'

'Oh, yes,' Alix said softly. 'Liam uses everything— and everyone.' For a moment she had an image of him, so blindingly vivid that he might have been standing beside her. She could almost feel the warmth of his body—taste the scent of his skin. Hurriedly she pulled herself together, making herself smile. 'I'll come and see you again in a few days.'

'Check before you do,' Margaret cautioned. 'I hope to be out of here before very long.' She smiled as she spoke, and Alix knew that in spite of the shock of her illness, and its consequences, the fabric of her life was still secure. She was thinking of her home, her husband, Debbie, and wanting to get back to them, and it gave Alix a greater than ever sense of isolation.

Even her stay with Gemma and David had brought its awkward moments. They had a good marriage and it showed in their jokes, their shared silences, the way they looked at each other, touched and smiled. Sometimes Alix was aware of an envy so deep that she had to turn away in case it showed nakedly on her face. How far she had sunk if she could actually be jealous of others' happiness, she thought bitterly.

Alix got up from her cushion, and drew the curtains to shut out the gathering darkness. She wasn't going to allow herself to sink into morbid self-pity, just because she was alone for an evening. She had a paperback thriller to read which actually seemed as if it was going to live up to its description, and later there was a play on television, a highly recommended repeat, which she had missed the first time around.

She switched on the television on her way back to the fireside, and found she had caught the last few minutes of a nightly magazine programme. She settled herself back on her cushion, reaching for her book, not really watching the screen, and only half listening to some Member of Parliament's opinion on a forthcoming by-election.

The interviewer was saying, 'We've been hearing about the possibility of a change of direction for a constituency, and today there's been news of a rather more personal change of direction for one of the great stars of our time.

'Bianca Layton, it has been announced, has turned down the role of Francesca in the forthcoming film of that name—a part that was widely rumoured might well be the crown on a career which has established her as one of the most popular actresses on both sides of the Atlantic. Instead, the role will go to a young unknown—Paola Minozza—and Bianca has announced that she will be playing the part of Francesca's mother, Irene.

'Good evening, Miss Layton,' he went on, turning in his chair. 'The news has caused something of a sensation, as you must be aware.'

The book slipped unnoticed from Alix's hand as she stared at the screen. Bianca was there, looking amazingly beautiful in a cream dress, with fox furs flung casually over her shoulder. She looked smiling and relaxed.

'I think a sensation must be rather an exaggeration,' she said. 'Yes, I've had a successful career, but it's also been a long one—too long, I feel, for me to play any more young girls with any degree of conviction.'

'Does that mean that you're abandoning your image as a sex-symbol?'

'It was never an image I consciously cultivated,' Bianca laughed, crossing exquisite legs. 'But who says that mature women can't be sexy? I'm sure there are a lot of wives, mothers—even grandmothers watching at this moment who could tell you a different story. I think it's time we all stood up and were counted.'

'What made you decide the time was ripe for a change?'

'I've had it in mind for some time,' Bianca said calmly. 'And during my reading of the *Francesca* script I became more and more attracted to playing Irene. It's a very strong role, written with great humanity and power, and it will be a considerable challenge after some of the lightweight material I've been offered in recent years. I've thoroughly enjoyed everything I've done,' she added, 'but I've now reached a stage where I need a change—perhaps even some serious purpose in my life. As you probably know, there's a book about my life and career in preparation at the moment, and this has caused me, naturally, to do some thinking about the past—and about the future too.' Her smile widened. 'You could say it's been a salutary experience.'

'So what are your immediate plans?'

'We're going to finish the book, I hope before filming starts on *Francesca*, and I plan to visit my family. I have a sister who's been ill, and I hope to spend some time with her. And . . .' she added with a mischievous upward look from beneath her lashes.

'And it's rumoured that there's a new romance in your life,' the interviewer prompted. 'Is it possible that you're going to take the plunge into matrimony again? You haven't had a great deal of luck with previous ventures.'

Bianca gave a deprecating shrug. 'I think I probably made my own luck. We're not making any definite announcement just yet, but I can say I'm very happy, and that I'm planning a wedding.'

'And are we allowed to speculate about the bridegroom's name?' The interviewer sounded arch.

'You could, but I can guarantee you'd be wrong,' Bianca returned. 'I can promise that the announcement when it comes will be a tremendous surprise.'

'We can hardly wait,' the interviewer said effusively. 'An intriguing note on which to end the programme. Thank you, Miss Layton.'

'Could I just add a personal note?' Bianca leaned forward, and the camera focussed on her in close-up, after a brief hesitation as if this unscripted addition had momentarily thrown a studio team, all geared up to roll the credits. Bianca was looking straight into the lens, and her green eyes were sparkling, but no longer with mischief. With something that looked incredibly like tears. She said, 'I have a message for my daughter—if she's watching. Alix—darling Alix, I need you. Please come back,' she ended on a husky note, as in the background the programme's signature tune could faintly be heard. The camera swung away, capturing for an instant the frozen look on the face of the interviewer, who had just realised that he had let the real sensation of the night get away. Then the figures faded into silhouette as the credits rolled over the screen.

Alix almost leapt across the room, her hand reaching shakily for the 'off' button. As the screen went blank, she stood in front of the set trembling like a leaf.

She lifted her hand, and laid her fingers across the quiver of her lips.

How could Bianca have done such a thing? But of course, she knew how. She was an actress, and she was playing a scene. She wasn't going to wait for the book to come out. She had decided to break the news that she had a daughter in her own time, and her own way.

And she was planning a wedding. Alix felt a little groan rise in her throat, as she remembered every word Bianca had said, every look, every gesture. Everything had stated her total satisfaction, both physical and emotional, with the new man in her life—the man whose identity was being kept secret for the time being, but which would prove such a surprise when it was made public. The man who, after all, knew all her secrets, and would never therefore suffer disillusions.

She wondered numbly exactly how much younger than Bianca Liam was. Probably not a great deal more than ten years, and that was hardly a shattering difference in this day and age. Probably they were waiting for the book to be finished before they made the actual announcement. The book which had brought them together in spite of everything.

And she needs me, Alix thought, letting the pain strike at her. What for? To make the arrangements, send out the invitations, book the honeymoon, act as bridesmaid? I can't ... oh God, I can't!

But of course Bianca didn't know what had happened between Liam and herself. She would assume that her warning had been sufficient, and that Alix would have been careful to keep him at arm's length ever since.

As I should have done, Alix thought bitterly. When we reached London, I should have run away, and kept running. I should have made sure that I never saw him again.

Well, at least she could make sure they never met again in the future, for both their sakes. Liam would have been as shaken by Bianca's appeal as she had been. If there was no response, then her mother would try and trace her through the Coulters, so she would have to leave Gemma and David as soon as possible. Anywhere would do as a refuge for the time being—a hostel, even a hotel room. She supposed she would be found eventually, but by that time Liam and Bianca would be married, and she would be sufficiently inured to the idea to be able to meet him without—oh God— without giving away completely her own love, her own longing. Surely there would come a time when she would be able to meet his eyes without the torment of knowing how much she desired him. A time when she would know she had finally broken free from this physical enslavement he had inflicted on her.

The cosy room suddenly seemed very cold. There was no way she could divert herself with books or television, she thought, wrapping her arms round her body. She would go upstairs and start her packing, and leave first thing in the morning.

Bianca wouldn't start looking for her tonight. She would be besieged by the press by now, which gave Alix some grace at least.

She was in the hall with her foot on the bottom stair when the doorbell rang. She paused, looking irresolutely over her shoulder. She could guess who it would be. Mrs Reynolds, Gemma's neighbour, was a kindly woman, but an inveterate gossip. She had found out that Alix had been Bianca's secretary, and been fascinated by the information. If it hadn't been for Gemma's firm intervention, she would undoubtedly have put Alix through a searching inquisition about her glamorous employer.

And television was Mrs Reynolds' passion. Unless by some miracle she had been watching the other channel, she had put two and two together and had come next door with the speed of light to check that her total was correct.

I can't simply ignore her, Alix thought helplessly. She knows Gemma and David have gone out because it's their anniversary, and she's seen the light on in the sitting room.

The bell rang again, a long imperative peal. Sighing, Alix went to the door and opened it. All she could do, she thought, as she lifted the latch, was claim total ignorance.

'Yes?' she began less than encouragingly as she faced her caller, then fell back a step, her face blanching. She grabbed at the door, trying to slam it, but Liam was too quick for her, and she was no match for his strength.

'Don't make a scene, Alix,' he advised coolly, as he shouldered his way into the hall. 'We're being observed. I saw curtains moving.'

'How—how did you find me?' Her mind was reeling. He was still at the television studios with Bianca. He had to be. She had counted on it.

'Not easily. I practically had to shake the information out of your little bitch of a cousin. I hope to God that unfortunate guy she's going to marry learns to handle her before it's too late, or his life will be a misery. Didn't she ever get slapped as a child?'

'I don't think either of us did.' This was madness, she thought dazedly, standing here discussing her upbringing and Debbie's with Liam. 'Did it ever occur to you that I didn't want to be found?'

'Yes, it did, but I wasn't going to let that stop me.' His eyes ran over her assessingly. 'You look like a ghost, secretary bird, and you've lost weight. Haven't these friends of yours been looking after you?'

'They've been wonderful,' she returned hotly.

'But not wonderful enough, clearly,' he said. 'I should have got back sooner, but it was impossible. The last week's been hell, as you can probably guess. But at least everything's sorted now.' He looked around him. 'Are you alone? Is there somewhere where we can talk?'

'Gemma and her husband are out, but they'll be back at any moment,' she lied. 'And we have nothing to talk about.'

'Oh, yes we have, Alix,' he said very quietly, and suddenly his eyes were on her mouth, and that cool, steady gaze was in some strange way as potent as a kiss, and she felt herself tremble.

'Then let me put it another way,' she said raggedly. 'There's nothing that I want to talk about—that I'm prepared to discuss with you. Will you please go, and leave me alone.'

She saw the firm lips tighten, and the dark brows draw together in a swift frown. There was a pause, then he said, 'Very well—but I presume your embargo doesn't also apply to Bianca. Surely you realise we have to talk about her?'

She had once heard someone say that hands were a dead giveaway of tension, and she knew hers were shaking, so she hid them behind her back.

She said, 'Are you afraid that I'll tell her what happened? I—I wouldn't, Liam. I don't want to spoil anything—for either of you. That's the truth, so you don't have to worry about anything any more.'

'I might appreciate your assurances more if I knew

what the hell you were talking about,' he said. 'One of the things I came here to say is that Bianca's back in the country, and she wants to see you.'

'I know she does.' Alix looked down at the pattern on the hall carpet. 'She—she said so on television just now.'

'Did she?' Liam began to smile. 'Then she kept her word. She promised that one of the first things she would do when she got back was acknowledge you as her child, and face whatever music resulted, but I admit I doubted her. She must want this marriage very badly.'

Her teeth sank into her lip. She said, 'You—you make it sound as if announcing that she had a grown-up daughter was—a—a condition.'

'And so it was,' he said sardonically. 'No man wants a wife who inhabits a fantasy world to the extent Bianca's been used to. Marriage needs a realistic approach if it's going to work.'

'And you think that this time it will work.' She felt as if every word was forced from her, but she had to go and play her part in this agony of a conversation. She must have more of Bianca in her than she had ever guessed.

'I think it has the best chance ever.' Liam looked at her, forcing her to meet his gaze. 'She's made the first move, Alix—belatedly, I agree—but can you meet her halfway? She can hardly plan our wedding without you being there,' he added, his mouth twisting slightly.

She could bear no more. 'Damn you,' she whispered fiercely. 'No, I won't meet her—plan your wedding. Do you think I have no feelings? Bianca's always treated me as if I was a cipher, but I won't take if from you, Liam. Perhaps in time I'll be able to forget—that night, but not yet. I've tried, and I'll go on trying, but I'm only human. And you taught me, Liam, you taught me to be a woman instead of just—just a secretary bird. Now go. Tell Bianca anything you like, but just go.'

She headed blindly for the stairs, but he caught her, turning her to face him.

'I've never thought of you as a cipher, Alix,' he said thickly. 'And I'm aware, more than aware, that you have feelings, even if they've not always been in line with my own. As for forgetting that I'm your lover, I want you to remember it every living, breathing moment that we have left to us. Oh, God—Alix!' He bent and kissed her mouth with a searching, demanding passion that had her yielding weakly in his arms.

When she could speak, she said, 'No, Liam—we can't. It's wrong, you know it is.'

'Darling, you're crazy!' he said on a note of shaky laughter. 'How can it be wrong, when it's so obviously, gloriously right? Don't pretend that you don't love me. I know you, Alix, and you couldn't have given yourself to me so perfectly, so completely, if you hadn't cared.' He groaned. 'I haven't had a night's sleep since, remembering how it was with us. I swore to Bianca I'd bring you back to the house tonight, but I can't. We've got to be together.' His voice sank to a whisper, and he kissed her again, deeply, tenderly.

At last she tore herself away. Her heart was pounding painfully, and her legs were shaking as she sank down on to a stair, leaning against the carved newel post.

She said, 'We can't do this to Bianca.'

He looked amazed, and then he began to laugh. 'Don't overestimate Bianca's new-found maternal instinct, my sweet. As long as I make you happy, and take these—' he touched the lines of strain around her mouth and the shadows beneath her eyes with a gentle finger '——away, she won't question too closely how I did it. Besides, she's far too involved in her reconciliation with Lester to care whether we anticipate our marriage vows.'

Her throat closed up with surprise. She said, 'Lester?' on a croak.

'Well, don't sound so surprised. From various comments you've made in the past, I'd gathered you were on his side, and would be pleased.'

Alix stared up at him. 'I don't understand.'

'It's quite simple,' he said. 'Lester arrived at the villa not long after our departure, and took charge. He and Bianca held a running battle which was still going when I arrived back, and told him that you now knew the truth about your parentage. Lester had always suspected that you were Bianca's child, because of the unexpected interest she took in you when you were younger. Yet she was totally indifferent to the younger girl, and this struck him as odd. When he suggested that she should employ you as her secretary, she was all for the idea, but after you arrived she started to have second thoughts, and this puzzled him, but every time he tried to question her, there was a terrible row. When I was able to tell him that the truth was out, he confronted her with it, and she just—crumpled.' Liam shook his head. 'It all came pouring out—her fears for her career, her terror of growing old, of becoming less desirable, the way she'd had to stop trusting people because they could turn out to be rivals at the least, or enemies at most. In some way she'd got it into her head that because she'd loved you but given you away to her sister, she had herself forfeited the right to be loved. And she'd also convinced herself that if the truth ever came out, everyone would turn against her in disgust. So all her life that poor creature has been rejecting people because she was terrified that one day she would be rejected.'

He paused. 'You can't do this to her, Alix. However wretched she's made you, however sore you may feel, you've got to give her the chance to make amends. She needs that.'

As he spoke a tiny bubble of happiness had begun to grow deep inside her, and now she thought she would explode with joy.

She said, 'I thought it was you—with Bianca—the wedding. You.'

'Oh God!' Liam reached down and drew her to her feet, holding her against him. 'You always did have this fixation about me having an affair with Bianca. There was never anything like that between us.' He gave her a searching look. 'You have to believe me, Alix. She's a beautiful, sexy woman, but I was there to ask questions for the book, not to get involved on any sort of level. I had this gut feeling that there was something in her past she didn't want me to know about—a feeling which my early encounter with you seemed to confirm. You, of course, were a total enigma. You put up this barrier and retreated behind it, and I kept trying to needle you—to break it down, to find the real girl, the one I saw on the stairs that day.'

Her mouth curved wryly. 'I think I loved you then, Liam, but I was so afraid. I thought you'd fall under her spell like they all did.'

'Perhaps I might have done,' he said. 'If I hadn't been bewitched already. I'd begun to think I was wasting my time until I pulled you out of the pool that day. Just for a moment you looked so happy, and I couldn't help wondering if that happiness was for me, so I kissed you, and when you responded so sweetly, I knew that one day you'd be mine.'

She sighed, remembering. 'I didn't know what to think. You treated me as if I was a child—as if I'd never been kissed before.'

'Nor had you—by me,' he said. 'Actually I was exercising the greatest restraint. There you were—in my arms and almost naked. I wanted to complete the process, and take you there and then, but I knew you weren't ready for that. I'd already gathered that you were—untouched, and I didn't want to spoil things or frighten you.'

Alix smiled. 'Bianca saw us and came to warn me about you.'

'So she told me. I've forgiven her. After all, at the time she had no reason to believe my intentions were honourable.'

Alix thought, 'And whether you know it or not, my darling, she wanted you for herself.' But she remained silent.

She said, 'Does Bianca know everything, then—including the fact that Lester was instrumental in stopping her getting the Francesca part?'

He nodded. 'There are no more secrets between them any more. They're going to remarry very soon, but on Lester's terms this time, and he intends to make her toe the line. I don't think he's actually quoted "Grow old along with me. The best is yet to be" at her yet, but it can only be a matter of time.' He paused. 'One of his terms was that she should frankly acknowledge you as her daughter, and resign herself to the nine-day wonder it will cause. After all, she's always lived her life in a blaze of publicity, not all of it good, so she can hardly jib now.' He grinned. 'Seb will find a way of putting the story over so that people are reaching for handkerchiefs rather than stones to throw.'

'Does this mean that you're still going to write the book?'

'Why not?' He shrugged slightly. 'There's nothing to stop me now. No more ghosts from the past or skeletons in her cupboard. Besides, she probably thinks that having her son-in-law as her biographer will give her some kind of control.'

'And could she be right?' There was a note of mischief in Alix's voice, answered by the smile in Liam's eyes as he looked at her.

'No, my darling, she's wrong. There's only one woman who has any hold over me, or any power to control how I live my life. She can practise her wiles and tantrums on Lester instead. He'll know how to deal with them.'

'Has she forgiven Leon yet?' Alix asked anxiously.

'Yes—he was summoned back to Italy for the signing of the contracts.'

She said slowly, 'And Monty? How has she taken the

news? She never liked me and . . .'

'Monty was the only other person who knew the truth from the beginning. It was she who rented the place in Northumberland where Bianca and her sister lived until you were born, and she looked after Bianca afterwards too. She didn't dislike you really. She simply adored Bianca and rejected anything that might harm her—a category into which you, my sweet, were instantly slotted. She was horrified when Bianca decided to take you into the household. She thought it was a sentimental act that would betray Bianca in the end. I don't think you'll find her so hostile in the future.'

She said ruefully, 'I keep telling myself I'm dreaming, but that any moment I'll wake up, and I'll be alone again.'

'I'll prove you're awake,' said Liam. 'I'll pinch you.' And did so, very softly and sensuously.

Alix gasped, and slid her arms up around his neck. The pressure of his hard body against hers was making her senses swim, and she had to concentrate in order to think coherently.

She said, 'When are you taking me to see Bianca?'

'Later,' he said huskily. 'It's selfish of me, Alix, I know, but I want you to myself for tonight at least. When the full story breaks none of us will have any peace for days, until the next sensation comes along. Do you think you'll be able to bear it?'

'I can bear anything,' she said, 'as long as I know that you love me.'

'I love you, Alix,' he said, then, wickedly, 'Want me to prove it?'

'By pinching me again?' she teased.

He kissed her, his mouth lingering on hers. 'Among other things. When did you say your friends would be back?'

'Not for hours,' she confessed. 'They're celebrating their wedding anniversary.'

'How very considerate of them!' He put his arm round

her, and began to walk with her up the stairs. 'This time next year, they can help us celebrate ours.'

Alix laughed shakily. 'You make it sound wonderful.'

'That,' he said, 'is because it will be wonderful. We'll make it wonderful for each other.'

'For the rest of our lives,' she said, and smiling with the promise of joy, she went willingly into his arms.

Harlequin® Plus

FETTUCCINE ALFREDO

When in Rome, do as the Romans do. Good advice, particularly when it comes to eating! One of the most delightful and popular Italian dishes is Fettuccine Alfredo. It's quick and easy to make—and delicious to eat!

What you need:

1 lb. fettuccine noodles
8 cups of water, salted
6 eggs
3 cups heavy cream
½ teaspoon salt
pepper to taste
2 cloves garlic, crushed
½ cup butter
1 cup grated Parmesan cheese
parsley, chopped

What to do:

In a large saucepan, bring water to a boil, add fettuccine noodles, partially cover and simmer for 7 to 10 minutes. Meanwhile, in a large bowl, thoroughly beat eggs and cream together with salt and pepper. Add garlic to mixture. When noodles are cooked—they should be slightly chewy—drain into a colander and run under cold water then under hot to remove starch and prevent noodles from becoming sticky. Turn noodles back into the saucepan, place on low heat and add butter. Stir until butter is melted. Add egg mixture and mix in until noodles are thoroughly coated. Add Parmesan and stir until cheese is well distributed. Turn into a large serving dish. Serves 6 to 8. *Buon' appetito!*

HELP HARLEQUIN PICK 1982's GREATEST ROMANCE!

We're taking a poll to find the most romantic couple (real, not fictional) of 1982. Vote for any one you like, but please vote and mail in your ballot today. As Harlequin readers, you're the real romance experts!

Here's a list of suggestions to get you started. Circle your choice, <u>or</u> print the names of the couple you think is the most romantic in the space below.

Prince of Wales / Princess of Wales

Luke / Laura (General Hospital stars)

Gilda Radner / Gene Wilder

Jacqueline Bisset / Alexander Godunov

Mark Harmon / Christina Raines

Carly Simon / Al Corley

Susan Seaforth / Bill Hayes

Burt Bacharach / Carole Bayer Sager

_____
(please print)

_____

_____

Please mail to: Maureen Campbell
Harlequin Books
225 Duncan Mill Road
Don Mills, Ontario, Canada
M3B 3K9

POLL-1

Take these best-selling
4 novels
FREE